Tuesday Meltdown

Joe D. Hinds

Copyright © 2014 Joe D. Hinds
All rights reserved.
ISBN-13: 978-1505891560
ISBN-10: 1505891566

DEDICATION

This book is dedicated to my wife Denise, the love of my life.

CONTENTS

    Acknowledgments   i

1	Not Just Another Day	Pg 1
2	Trouble at Home	Pg 7
3	Family, Friends, and Plans	Pg 9
4	Marauders	Pg 21
5	New Neighbors	Pg 29
6	DHS at Bo Hill	Pg 63
7	Christmas Rescues	Pg 77
8	The Hungry Horde	Pg 95
9	Sabotage at Riceland Railhead	Pg 105
10	Second Battle of Oak Ridge	Pg 109

ACKNOWLEDGMENTS

I would like to recognize my family's role in the writing of this book. My father and mother always were there for me and fostered my love for reading. My sons inspired this book in more ways than they will know. Finally, I would like to simply point upward to Him who has tolerated my stupidity for so long, He has to love me. Otherwise I would not be here today.

1 NOT JUST ANOTHER DAY

    Jason Hamilton had no idea he would be involved in a gun battle that Tuesday. It seemed like another ordinary morning. Jason drank his coffee and turned on the news. Good Morning America reported that the Chinese Yuan had replaced the U.S. Dollar for global trading. The U.S. government had announced it would no longer prop up Wall Street. Finally, the stock market had plunged into the 5,000 territory. The world was a mess, but Jason didn't need to see the news to know that. He simply drank his morning coffee and kissed his wife goodbye.

    For Jason, Tuesday was a workday as a public school teacher. Although three months earlier the government had confiscated his school retirement savings, Jason still had a job. Sometimes that job seemed a thankless one, but Jason felt like he was making a difference. So for today, while China was demanding immediate payment of the U.S trade deficit, Jason was teaching his students the Constitution's Bill of Rights. Elsewhere in America there was civil unrest, but the buses were still running at Tuckerville Intermediate School.

    After lunch, however, it became evident something had changed. School had been dismissed early without an explanation. As Jason pulled out of the parking lot, he noticed things were different. There were lines at the gas stations. People were filling up empty gas cans and barrels. A police car seemed to be at every gas station, and although the price was still $3.14 a gallon, and things were peaceful, it was apparent that there would be a fuel shortage in the next few days. Driving by the local Wal-Mart, he noticed the parking lot was full. Jason actually wanted to stop by and get a movie from Redbox, but this seemed like too much of a hassle. Instead he decided he would simply drop in and see what was going on. Two ladies were in the parking lot, cursing obscenities at each other. One woman was in tears. Approaching the front door, Jason noticed the sign: "We ask that you please limit your food purchases to $50 or less." Underneath, an 8½ x

11 inch piece of paper read: "We can currently only accept cash purchases. We apologize for the inconvenience." Jason left the store before going in, not quite catching the disruption occurring in the packed checkout lines. He ran to the car, and drove across the parking lot to the bank ATM. It was still operational. He took out his seven hundred dollar limit from his Bank of America account and was able to complete a 900-dollar transaction from a credit card account as well. Trying his second credit card, a prompt appeared on the screen: "Your transaction cannot be completed at this time. We apologize for the inconvenience."

On the way home, he called his wife Deborah. She answered with her sweet playful voice, "Well, hello there." How could the simple sound of her voice make all trouble seem distant? After he and his first wife divorced, Jason had somehow found Deborah. Deborah had been the one reason that kept Jason going through those hard times.

"Hi, baby," Jason responded, sounding like a dumbstruck teenager. Collecting his thoughts, he continued, "Hey baby, there is a big line at Wal-Mart and at the gas stations. I took out all the cash I could from my bank account and managed to get some from the Visa." She was going to think he was on his SHTF kick again.

"I could be wrong, but I think something is going on. I can always pay the money back, right?"

"Umm...I guess."

"I'm on my way home. Please don't go anywhere." A pause. "I love you, baby."

"I love you, too, honey."

On the way home, Jason saw more traffic than usual going toward town. On a whim, Jason turned right instead of left. Why not visit Sunshine Grocery, the local Mennonite store?

As he pulled up to the store, Jason noticed a red Dodge Ram parked in front of the store entrance with both doors open. A young man in his early twenties was backing out of the door and holding something...a shotgun. A muffled pop, a scream inside. Jason instinctively reached under his seat for his snub-nosed revolver. He had originally chosen this revolver as a backup weapon to his 9mm Browning, but now he found himself carrying the revolver in his car wherever he went. One could never tell when something might happen. Apparently something was happening now. A red-headed woman carrying a small revolver appeared behind the young man. She shouted to her male accomplice, and he turned to face Jason. The young lady fired at Jason, punching a spider-webbed hole in his windshield. The young man wheeled his shotgun toward Jason, when Jason fired his snub-nose twice. The first shot went high, hitting the glass door, shattering it. The second nailed the apparent thief in the stomach. The red head screamed, dropped the bag she had been holding, and pushed the injured man into the truck. She hopped in the driver's side, and peeled out, throwing rocks as they left.

Staring down the road in disbelief, Jason was lost in the moment. This was unreal. All of it. Remembering the scream, Jason followed his gun inside, shouting out a warning that he was there to help. Inside he found a Mennonite woman kneeling on the ground, her black and white patterned dress stained with red. She was crying and holding her stomach, screaming she had been shot. Jason ran to her, instructed her to lay down, when the humor hit him. Ketchup. The would-be thieves had shot the condiment tray next to the lady. Perhaps the lady would suffer hearing damage and some emotional trauma, but she would be okay.

After calming the store cashier down, he discovered her name to be Mrs. Maxine Berger. Jason called his wife, telling her what had happened. No, he was okay. No, she should stay at home. He would be back after the police came. The 911 operator said it would be a while, but they would send someone over.

When Mr. Burger arrived, he insisted on Jason calling him Harold. He offered that Jason take whatever he wanted from the store--free of charge. Jason was thankful yet politely declined, stating that he would pay a fair price. Harold indicated that he lived across the road, pointing to a modest house about a quarter mile out surrounded by pasture where goats and sheep were grazing. As they both waited for the police, the two talked.

"Some of my church says it's the end times. Satan has filled this country with greed and all sorts of sexual immorality," Harold remarked. "Now I don't know about all of that," Harold continued. "I do know a man has to be prepared for both God and men," thumping his shotgun with his Bible. Jason wholeheartedly agreed. It was evening before he was heading home. Next to him was a 2-liter Coke and his revolver. In the truck behind him was a new friend along with 6 goats and 5 sheep Jason had purchased. The price: eight hundred two dollars and 37 cents. It had seemed like a good deal for both of them.

The news on television that evening was not good. First, the U.S. dollar became essentially worthless for trade. As a result, trade with Southeast Asia and Europe was at a virtual standstill overnight. Also oil imports could not be purchased with dollars, which promised to slow petroleum production. Although the U.S. had many domestic sources of oil and natural gas, these had been pitifully underdeveloped. Stores relying on mass transportation could not be stocked. Regarding Wall Street, the stock market was yet to reopen.

The local news channel for the nearby city of Middleton, KVLN 6, reported looting at Kmart on Southland Drive. The Wal-Mart in Middleton had taken the extreme measure of hiring private security armed with shotguns. As a result, one person had been shot and was listed in critical condition at St. Mary's. Finally, most public schools in Northeast Arkansas were reported as being closed for that next day.

Jason and Deborah talked that evening. As a nurse, Deborah was expected to work. Babies still had to be delivered, right? The only problem was that gasoline was reported being in scarce supply. Should she continue to work when there was no guarantee that she could refill the car? The second topic of discussion was essentials. Where Jason had planned for possible emergency situations, there were still lots of unanswered questions. Jason had been storing up dry goods for the last few years to the extent that everyone in his family thought he had been a bit off his rocker. Whether it was learning how to arc weld, digging his own well, or learning to trap wild game, he had always been preparing. There was enough dried beans, rice, and cornmeal to last at least 6 months. He and Deborah had rabbits, chickens, goats, sheep, and even a cow/calf pair. What had before been a convenient and practical tax write-off now appeared to be quite essential.

Even though they had made some preparations for such an event as this, there were always unanswered questions. Would the power go out? If so, would the power bill be so high as to run them out of money? How would they pay the bills if they could not get to work? Would cell phone service last?

The answer: They did not know. It was late September, and the question of heat came up. How would they survive if they had no electricity and could not refill their propane? Jason did have the propane tank full and several 20 lb containers that they normally used for grilling. Deborah agreed that they should look into a wood stove for the living room. The place for a wood stove was already there, wood boxes on each side, chimney and all. Simply no stove. But where to find one, especially now?

Jason locked up the gate that night thinking about the events of the day: of the attempted robbery and of the two ladies fighting outside Wal-Mart. If people had no food to eat, how would they act? How long would it be before those hungry people grew violent? When he got back inside, Jason expressed his concern to his wife, and reluctantly she agreed to call in sick that next day. Just to see how things would turn out.

Jason and Deborah spent much of Wednesday at home. On the news, it was reported that debit and credit cards would not work. Somehow this was linked to the banks, which had invested in the stock market. Apparently, EBT cards, formally known as food stamps, still worked if the store would accept them. Many major retailers were reporting problems with the U.S. government reimbursing EBT expenses. According to a radio news broadcast, the President had issued an executive order that all stores must continue to accept EBT. Some stores, however, were ignoring that order. In short, the news was not getting any better.

That afternoon, Jason and Deborah had visitors walking up their driveway. A Hispanic man and his wife, holding a baby, came asking for food for their baby and perhaps a ride. Their car had run out of gas on the highway about three miles out of Oak Ridge, and no one would help them.

Deborah came out with two cans of condensed milk and a cup. The young Mexican woman was thankful, expressing herself in a dialect incomprehensible to Deborah that nevertheless expressed profound gratitude. Pouring the opened can of milk in the cup, the woman doused the end of a cloth diaper in it and placed it next to the child's mouth, who hungrily latched onto the meal. Speaking with the man, Jason agreed to give them a ride at least to the county line. He could use that time to check on his new friend, Harold. Grabbing his SKS and snub-nosed revolver, he and the family got into his old red Oldsmobile Alero and started down the drive. Jason smiled as he thought about his humble ride. At least his vehicle would probably not be the first to be carjacked.

Along the way, Jason noticed other cars on the side of the road, abandoned. When he passed the old winery road, he noticed a farmer that had blocked the road with some farm equipment. The farmer was holding a rifle. Apparently, that road was closed. Farther down at the junction, which turned toward Tuckerville, Jason could see blue police lights in the distance. Well, he wasn't going down there anyway. Rather than drop them off at the county line, Jason drove Juan, his wife, and child the extra 5 miles home. When they arrived at their trailer, Juan was extremely grateful and invited Jason in for rice and beans, but Jason politely declined. He needed to check on Harold and get back home.

The Mennonite store was not open, and at first glance, no one seemed to be home at the Berger residence. Only when Jason pulled into the drive did he see the two young men, with rifles raised. Then Harold walked out, raised his hand, and told his boys to lower their guns. Evidently, someone else had tried to rob the store a second time. Harold had decided it would be safer to simply close up shop. Jason listened and nodded. When he explained how he had helped Juan and his family, Harold listened politely and shook his head.

Harold spoke simply and directly: "God expects you to provide for your family, Jason. You cannot rightfully provide for them if you are dead, now can you?" Jason looked at him puzzled, and Harold continued. "Mr. Jason, this morning I killed a man who tried to rob my store. Until then, I had never taken to violence against any man. Now two people have been shot at my store in the last two days. The police never came yesterday, and there was no answer when I called today. It would seem we are on our own for a while."

Jason told him of his concern about the electricity. Harold agreed. "Electric may not last more than a few more days, maybe not even today. I tell you what I got." The old man led Jason around to the back yard, leaving his two boys to stand guard. "It's yours if you want it. I still owe you for saving my wife, and I was raised to owe no man anything." Jason followed Harold into a rather large wooden shed. Back in the corner, covered with a dusty sheet, was a Peacock wood stove.

"Umm, I don't have a truck."

"It comes apart at the base. If you put your seats down, you may be able to fit it in. The base can go in your trunk I think, if you tie it down. It is heavy, though."

Jason told Harold his concern about security at the house as they loaded the stove. "You got sons, don't you? Call 'em home to you; help them out, but trust no one else. Times are gonna get rough, most likely. I hope I am wrong."

As they finished loading the stove, Harold placed his hand on Jason's shoulder in a firm yet gentle manner, staring him in the eyes. "Now go. Take care of your family. God *will* be with you." Mr. Berger had spoken the last sentence like a pronouncement of an undeniable fact.

2 TROUBLE AT HOME

    Going home was not simply quiet; it seemed to be a deathly calm. For one thing, there was no oncoming traffic. On the radio, a conservative talk show host blamed the Democratic administration for this failure. Jason wasn't worried about whom to vote for in the election, though, so he turned the radio off. At the Tuckerville Junction, the police lights were still about 2 miles distant, perhaps on the Ditch 26 bridge. The farmer on the Old Winery road was still standing there, blocking the road. Thinking of stopping, Jason slowed, looked out the window at the man, and decided stopping would not be wise. Jason nodded as he passed. The old man nodded back with a stoic face.
    When Jason approached his driveway, he noticed a white van at the gate. Stopping the car, Jason locked and loaded his SKS and moved behind the trees toward the gate. As he got closer, Jason observed his wife on the front porch with the shotgun in her hand. A man had just climbed over the gate and was talking with his hands up. Deborah was obviously nervous and confused. With a voice near tears, she was yelling at the man to leave, but the man, a large, rather obese fellow, kept advancing slowly. As Jason moved along the trees bordering the drive, he noticed the semiautomatic pistol stuffed in the back of the man's pants. Jason's mind raced. Were they law officers? No, not a chance. Whoever they were, they were up to no good. Jason unfolded the SKS's bayonet to the upright position.
    Approaching the van undetected, Jason encountered a second man, rather thin and pale, working the action of a deer rifle while opening the van's passenger door. Jason silently greeted the thin gentleman with cold steel in the throat as the man was stepping out of the van. A gurgle from his mouth and surprise in his eyes, the man eased to the ground as Jason took

the gentleman's rifle with his other hand. Jason eased to the front of the van, resting his weapon on it, and shouted a command to the remaining trespasser. "Drop to the ground, sir, or I will kill you where you stand." The overweight fellow did drop to the ground, grabbing the pistol from his pants and firing. The shot hit the van's headlight right next to Jason. Jason squeezed off three rounds with steady aim at the target on the ground. As the explosions rang out, at least one of the three rounds had hit the fat man squarely in the head. The 7.62 x39mm round did not leave much of the man's face. A smell of gunpowder lingered, and Jason's ears still rang as he realized he had killed two men. He ran to Deborah, who stood on the porch, shotgun still raised, weeping. He lowered her weapon and held her close. He had defended his wife. He had done the right thing. Supposing a call to 911 was in order, Jason was greeted by a computer voice saying all circuits were busy.

At the same time, Deborah had decided to call her daughter Haley. The tension in her face was somewhat relieved when Haley answered. She was with Tim at their house about thirty miles away. When Jason spoke to them, he told them if they were willing to make the trip, they were welcome. Take the dump truck, as much fuel, cash, and food that would fit in the back, and get here. Blankets and candles if they had 'em, but leave within the hour. They were not to stop for anyone.

Jason then tried to call his sons. He managed to reach his middle son, Philip. "Son, it is bad, and will most likely get worse." Philip and his brother, Peter, were willing to come over. Jason told him to simply come over with Peter in his truck, but they should leave immediately. "And turn off on Elm Grove Road," Jason told Phil, remembering the blue lights. "Do not stop for anyone, no matter what."

Jason and Deborah paused to examine their would-be invaders. Apparently, the men in the white van, now laying dead on the ground, had made another stop before coming to visit the Hamilton residence. In the back of the van were 4 plastic totes filled with canned food, cash inside a plastic grocery bag, and a 52" television. Also, wrapped in blankets were two shotguns, a .38 pistol, boxes of shotgun shells, and an El Paso Salsa tin, filled with .38 shells. It was 4:30 p.m.

3 FAMILY, FRIENDS, AND PLANS

"What do we do about the bodies?" Deborah asked. They both had begun taking the food, blankets, and guns inside the house. The 52" screen LCD Sanyo stayed in the van. "Baby, I am going to fall this second tree across the neighboring property so I can control access to the house. I need you to watch out for me with the gun while I do this. Are you up for this?" Deborah nodded, keeping watch as Jason got the chainsaw and started down the drive. In short order, he fell a tree down by the road, effectively cutting off the neighboring property to the wood line, making the driveway the only easy access to their property. He pulled the white van over to the side of the driveway and waited for his family to arrive.

About 20 minutes later, with rifles in hand, Jason and Deborah greeted their sons at the driveway. "Here son, take this," handing Philip a shotgun "Loaded with slugs." He handed Peter a Ruger 10/22. "Son, here is a 30 round magazine, and 2 ten rounders. You can load two more magazines this evening."

Jason and Deborah looked at their sons, who could not take their eyes off of the two bodies in the driveway. Deborah looked to Jason. "Jason, what are we gonna do with those men."

"I have no idea. Can't rightfully bury them. The police need to see what happened. We can let them lay here for now. It may let others know to go somewhere else instead of stopping here for easy pickings."

Jason's mind was racing. First and foremost was about his stepdaughter. Were they going to make it? Deborah was calling her now. She had just received the text that someone had shot at them going through Oak Ridge. They were okay. It would be about 10 minutes.

"Did you have any problem going through Elm Grove?" Both boys shook their head. Jason talked to his sons. They were understandably concerned about their friends in town. Jason explained that for now, the best place for everyone was to be with their families. Holding them both, Jason was thankful simply to have his two sons here with him, yet he still worried about his oldest son.

Phil and Jason busied themselves with unloading the stove into the living room while Deborah and Peter watched the road. About the time they had unpacked the last piece in the living room, the distinctive roar of a diesel engine caused both Jason and Philip to run out the front door. Sure enough, it was Haley and Tim. Deborah ran to her daughter, embracing her while Jason took note of the three bullet holes on the driver's side of the cab. "Damned near got me. This one flew through the cab. Almost got Haley." Jason handed Tim the confiscated deer rifle. "Happy birthday, Tim. Welcome on board. Did you manage to bring anything?"

"Food. We sort of threw everything in sheets and just slung it in the back. Watch out for the glass. Broke a bottle of Vodka."

Jason eyed the equipment in the bed of the 18-yard dump truck. "Generator?"

"Welder and generator. Runs off diesel. Got any?"

"Some. How much does this truck have?"

"Full."

That night, the group took assessment of their situation. "We have electric and water for now. The tubs are full. The hot tub is full. We do have a pond and a well down by the shed. The water may need to be boiled before we can drink it, though. And we may need a hand pump if the power goes out. Plus we need lamps and candles."

"How long do you expect this to last?" Peter asked.

"I don't know, son. I do know that water and power won't last long if the equipment is not maintained."

"Do we have food?"

"We may have enough. I bought some more livestock yesterday on a whim. We should save the animals for now."

"We can fish. Right, Dad?"

"Sure, in this pond and the one next door. We have to be ready, though. It is already dangerous. I can only imagine what will happen if people start to get hungry."

It was time to relieve Phil on watch. Peter would watch next. Two hour shifts. It was getting late, and they were tired. On the bright side, Jason was pretty sure that there was no school the next day.

It was morning, and the power was still on. The red digits on the clock glowed 5:12 a.m. Deborah got up, made coffee, and went out to see her husband, who was keeping watch. The morning air was cool and slightly damp. There would be dew this morning.

Handing her husband a cup of coffee, she then stood behind him, holding his waist. Although Jason had been caught up in thoughts of what might happen, just his wife's presence could bring him back to the simple pleasures of the moment. Perhaps it was her smile, the way her hair fell on her shoulders, or her easy laugh that made him realize that she was his reason for living. Whatever it was, just her being there with him made Jason feel alive. And this morning, in the predawn quiet, they were together.

"Tired, Hun?"

"Not really, baby. It's all quiet. Been that way all night from what I understand."

"Wanted to put on some eggs and bacon. Does that sound good?"

"Sounds great, baby. I wanted to see Robert Everling today and see about getting some rice. He should have his bins full about this time of year... I hope."

Jason understood that the best chance of surviving whatever was going on out there was to keep a low profile. This meant avoiding travel—especially to stores. Yet some travel was necessary. Six people meant much more food was needed. That meant crossing over to Robert's farm.

Over breakfast, the family talked about the day. "How long are we going to have electricity?" "What about internet?" "Phone service?"

"Thank God none of us are sick or needing medications," Haley added. Haley had been studying to be a nurse, like her mother.

"Like it or not, Tim, you are the maintenance guy." Jason announced. "We have a dump truck, a truck, two cars, and a van...at least for right now. Plus your generator and my tractor. What would you need to keep that and the mowers and such running for a long period of time?"

"We are going to need some fuel, for sure, if we are going anywhere. Plus tools, if something breaks down. And parts."

"Well I would appreciate it if you could just spend the morning looking around the place. I mean, my tools are a mess. Deborah, if you are okay with it, I could use you in the kitchen. It would be good to ration our food as if this is going to be a longer-term emergency." Emergency. It was the first time that word was spoken.

That morning on ABC's Good Morning America, George Stephanopolis was downplaying the idea that this was an emergency. Parroting the president, George was telling the American public to remain calm, and was somehow still blaming the Republicans for the failure of the government Supplemental Nutrition Assistance Program. Formerly called "food stamps," the government changed the name along with the look, offering recipients a sleek new card. It had been so successful that the current president had succeeded in impoverishing 15 million more people by enrolling them on the program. In other news, China had boarded American merchant vessels in international waters, confiscating the contents. America's Pacific fleet was ordered to maneuvers near Taiwan.

So much for good news.

Philip had wanted to go with his dad, but he was needed with the chainsaw. There was wood to cut and move. "Son, we need this stacked on the front porch, not out back. This wood has to double as sandbags against incoming fire. If something like yesterday happens again, we need cover. Needs to be chest high for you," Jason said, putting his arm across his chest. "Cut it in place, and we can carry it this afternoon."

Peter and Haley were to keep watch on both sides of the house. Everyone was to be armed. "Son," Jason grabbed Peter's shoulder. "I know you have never shot at anyone, but yesterday those two men tried to kill us. People are desperate. They will do anything. They may say they have children, or old people that are hurt. That might be true, but if they get close enough to talk to you, they are close enough to kill you and the girls. Understand? Can you do it?"

"Dad, I have to shoot them, right?"

"If it comes to that, yes son. They may be hungry, desperate, and afraid; but they will kill you. If you start shooting, we will all be there for you. Now stay lying here and just be ready."

Jason and Tim took Phil's truck, passing the bodies as they drove down the drive. Tim jumped out, moved the van to the road, allowing Jason to drive the truck through. Then Tim replaced the van, in effect sealing off the drive. As Jason drove past Bo Henderson's place next door, he realized what a gap in security that front yard was. Bo had been working construction and had not returned in the last 4 days. It was only a matter of time before someone discovered the place and ransacked it. And when they did, they would discover the gap on the north side of Jason's property. How could they close that gap? Wire? No way. Too much frontage to cover. As he passed Bo's place, he noticed the fire engines. Now that would make a hell of a roadblock. Hmm. So much to think about, so little time.

Not wanting to drive too fast to worry anyone, yet not wanting to drive too slow to present an easy target, Jason kept it about 40 mph as he approached the gravel road. Actually Pine View Road was only a half-mile from the house, and Jason could have cut off a mile of travel simply by taking the field behind his house. There was, however, a deep creek separating their place from that field. Coming back, he might park the truck at the edge of the field and maybe camouflage it. Might need a quick get away? Or maybe a way to stay off the main roads?

Driving down the road, it appeared to be a beautiful day. The cotton was blooming; the sun was shining. Jason resisted the urge to turn on talk radio. He had to stay focused. He had the SKS with him and a .22 single action revolver. He had left the 9mm semiautomatic with Tim, so he could be ready to back up the kids. (Hell, Tim was a kid himself, only 19.) As he got closer to the farm, Jason thought if Robert wanted him dead once he got there, he would be an easy target. It had been 20 years since he had spoken to Robert. The farmer had then loaned Jason a dump truck to help clean up a piece of property. Would Robert even recognize him? Jason drove the truck slowly and honked his horn to get someone's attention. Then he waited at the side of the gravel road, with his hands up in the air so they could see he meant no harm.

Robert and his son stepped out. The old farmer was unarmed, but his son Ronnie had what appeared to be an AR-15 trained on Jason. "Hey Robert. Hey Ronnie. Just came over to say hi and see if you had any rice I could get. Would love to buy some." Robert laughed, and Ronnie lowered the rifle.

Jason drove the truck to the back, and they talked at the tailgate. End times, if not for the world, at least it seemed bad for the U.S. No time was spent bad-mouthing the president or Congress. Problems seemed beyond placing blame. "What you need more than rice is dogs. Or guineas. A good dog or a guinea is the best alarm for anyone trying to sneak up on you." Robert had about 35 years of experience over Jason so Robert talked, and Jason listened.

Robert took Jason around back. "Got any containers?" Jason pointed to his 5 gallon buckets. "I thought I could get some of these filled." "Sure, but you could fill up a couple of these," Robert pointed to two 55 gallon water containers. Jason simply nodded. Jason placed the containers in the bed of his truck and drove up to the elevator.

"I reckon this rice will be better off here than trying to take it to the mill," Robert remarked as he filled one container, moving the nozzle to the next.

"How much will that be? I have money."

"Well, I figured you would. I never reckoned you as someone who took without paying. You have about 750 pounds of rice there. Now that's about .20 cents a pound, what I normally charge to deer hunters. That's $150 dollars."

Jason reached into his wallet, counted out $200 and gave it to Robert. Robert took it, then put the twenties into his other hand and handed Jason back the money. "You paid. Now I am giving you the money back. We have more than enough, anyway."

Robert continued: "Jason, I am thinking we ain't staying here. Ronnie has a place in the hills about 40 miles from here if we can make it. We are going there until the United States can pull its head from out of its rear end. I tell you what. My daughter has some hens and a rooster. If you want 'em, you can have em. I don't reckon they will travel very well. I don't have a pen to put 'em in, but you can take the chicken wire for later. We might be able to place them inside a tow sack or sheet or something."

Jason thanked Robert profusely. Robert replied, "You just keep your family safe. I may be back, Lord willing. It just depends on how things play out." Jason secured his two large barrels, jumped in the GMC Sonoma, and did turn on the radio, if for no other reason than to drown out the cackling of 5 hens and a large rooster on the cab's passenger side. When Robert and Jason had caught them, the birds made known that they weren't going in that sheet without a fight. "I don't have to worry about thugs ambushing me," Jason muttered to himself. "With all that noise, I'll be lucky if I don't drive off the road." Bull Weber was on the air, which meant that Jason had been gone for two hours. Now if he could just make it home.

Weber apparently was not in the entertainment mode, but rather that of a news reporter. Riots were taking place in Chicago, and fires were burning unchecked on the south side of the city for over twenty-four hours. Jason was not surprised that good ole George had not reported that this morning on ABC. New York City had declared marshal law, with a strict curfew being imposed. Apparently a large group of war veterans had been protesting at the White House. Tear gas and rubber bullets had been used to attempt dispersing the crowd. Somehow, live ammunition had come into use, and 34 veterans had been killed. Rumors of flash gang violence occurring in Cincinnati and Detroit had been confirmed by Fox News but discounted by the other networks. MSNBC accused Fox of race-baiting.

Jason turned off the radio, pulled on the paved road, and topped the ridge by Mr. Henderson's place to see for the second time in two days someone again in his drive. This time it was a police car. The lights were on, and crouched behind the white van, was a single police officer.

Jason pulled over to the side of the road, and with his SKS raised, he instructed the officer to step away from the vehicles, drop his weapon, and approach the road. With the rifle still trained on the cop, Jason stated calmly "What seems to be the problem, officer?" The officer, an obvious veteran of the force, replied he had been checking on the neighborhood, and that there had been reports of looting. Jason informed him that two would-be looters were laying up at the top of their drive. If he were there to make a report, he would be more than welcome to come up to the house as long as he could excuse the rifle being trained on him. The officer said he understood.

Jason and the officer walked to the drive, shouting at Peter. Peter and four other heavily armed people stood up. Jason was proud. While the policeman was filing his report, Jason got the "down-low" from Peter. Apparently, Peter had taken his father's instruction seriously, and the officer had almost been hit by the first blast from the 12 gauge. That had been followed by everyone dropping their work and running to assist the 18-year-old to defend their home.

"Well, honestly, this needs to be investigated, but we are undermanned with everything that is going on. I have no idea when I could have you come down. And there is still the matter of shooting at a police officer."

"Officer Henry, is it? With all due respect, I have to be honest with you. My family and I have been attacked twice in the two days before you came. Things have changed recently, and I pray they get better. Until that time, I will be here to defend my family. How is your family doing if I may ask?"

The veteran officer made a tight grimace. "I don't know. I live in West Memphis, and my wife hasn't answered my calls recently."

"You have a decision to make then, sir. Personally, I would take that cruiser of yours right now to your place and make things right. If your family needs a place to stay, we could always use your experience out here. I haven't heard about West Memphis yet, but Memphis is a wreck."

The stout officer shook Jason's hand. "I do not see any wrongdoing here," he said as he stepped over the two dead would-be thieves. "I have to be going. Let me get your number if I could...Jason, isn't it?" The police officer walked down the hill to his cruiser, backed out of the drive, and headed south.

Peter was sitting down on the ground. He was visibly shaking. Jason knelt down beside him, placing his hand over his shoulder. "Not like playing video games, is it?" Peter shook his head. Philip was standing next to the light pole with his arms crossed. He had managed to secure his 12 gauge shotgun from Peter, which the two had traded during morning watch. Underneath that false bravado, however, Jason knew that Philip was shaken, too. In fact, they all were. Jason went to his wife and held her. She seemed to be doing OK, considering the events of the last few days. It was time for a good meal...

The meal consisted of beans and bacon, (with a little bit of jalapeno pepper) and cornbread fried on the skillet. The boys ate heartily, while Haley picked at her food.

Tim finally spoke up. "You need more sockets and wrenches if I need to do any big job. Also, I was looking for a saw for cutting wood."

"Doesn't the chainsaw work?" Jason responded. "Are we out of gas?"

"Naw, that's not the problem. I just was thinking that running a chainsaw is telling someone two things driving down the highway. Number one: You are here, and Number two, you're working, not ready to fight."

That was a good point, Jason thought. He had often seen the two-man crosscut saws hanging on walls. The thought reminded him of his time up in Canada working with his brother. A two-man crosscut saw could even make two contentious teenage brothers work together as a team. The thought brought back old memories. Hmm.

"Good point. Right now I am thinking that the heavy work of falling wood comes first, though. If "Gunfights at the Hamilton Corral" are going to be a daily routine, I want that front porch holding 6 cords of firewood at least."

"How is the wood coming, son? Philip had worked hard that morning, getting some timber dropped. Honestly, Jason was happy his son still had two arms and legs still attached. That's when Jason noticed the scratches on Philip's hands and arms. He had to make sure his sons had proper gloves and shirts to work in the woods. Philip's shirt was torn in many places, and he needed to get some iodine on those cuts.

While hearing what Philip had to say about the wood, Jason suddenly remembered the chickens. Philip excused himself to relieve Peter on guard and Jason went out back to check on the truck. Were they still alive? Opening the door, Jason was greeted by one large red, black, and white rooster who had managed to get out of the sheet. He flew out the door with a ruckus. The hens were still safe inside. Thirty minutes of Jason and Tim running and chasing yielded no results in catching the stubborn bird, and only succeeded in making him louder. Both Deborah and Haley had a well-needed laugh while watching the affair. Finally giving up, Tim and Jason reconstructed the chicken pen under the shed awning. Placing the hens inside, Tim brought out a large bookcase, and lined it with lawn trimmings. The entire time, the rebellious rooster remained up in a nearby tree, keeping a watchful eye. "Maybe the rooster could serve as an alarm," Jason conceded, deciding to let the old bird alone in his perch.

In the front yard, Peter was bringing around the ladder and placing it against the back of a large oak tree that bordered the property. Peter climbed it to the first limb, where he found a perfect spot to perch the shotgun. Jason was surprised at his youngest son's tactical insight. The tree was rooted at the military crest of the ridge, not quite visible from the road, and the large trunk well shielded the ladder from potential enemy fire. Jason climbed the ladder and sure enough, all the front pasture was perfectly visible, including Bo's place a few hundred yards away. Jason got the confiscated .308 deer rifle from the house and handed it to Peter. "Don't be up there all the time, son." Jason gave Peter a piece of rope. "Tie off, too. And remember what you were taught about keeping an empty chamber."

Jason walked toward the troubling north side of the property. The pond's levee might make a suitable defense. Where some trees on one side of the property might have made a great LP/OP, there was no good avenue of regress if trouble came. Jason decided the second sentry post would be by a split oak, by far the largest tree on the property. Although its field of fire was partially obstructed by the shed, it offered visibility of the entire back of the house, easy regress to the house, and was in line-of-site with the tree position Peter had discovered. Clearly, plans for home defense were in order...as well as lots of practice. What Jason wouldn't do for a couple of TA 312 military field phones. If (when) the cellphones went out, there would be a communication problem.

Tim was getting the tractor's front end loader lined up with Philip's truck to unload the rice. After the two managed to maneuver both rice barrels under the carport, Jason mentioned the problem to Tim. "Well, we don't have crank-phones, but we do have quite a bit of wire around the house. See all that old telephone line on the shed down there. It runs underground. They had a telephone down at the shed."

"I am pretty sure we could rig up a battery-powered light system for people standing watch. Or a buzzer."

"You might be able to rig up a telephone of sorts if you have a microphone or a compact speaker," Tim responded.

"Hell. Walkie talkees would be great. You know, I actually tried to be prepared for something like this but apparently I should have thought this out more."

"It is what it is, huh?"

"Yeah."

Thoughts of the last two gun battles were on Jason's mind. He thought back to when he had visited the Alamo in San Antonio. Jason recalled Colonel Travis's plan was not holing up in that church. The Colonel had expected reinforcements. When that did not pan out, Travis had sought terms from the Santa Anna and received none. No terms nor quarter was offered. Indeed, virtually everyone at the place had died. They had had no chance. At the Alamo, 200 people could not hold 4 acres of Texas real estate. The idea that Jason's family could hold 7 acres against a determined, organized force was silly. Jason needed a "Plan B."

The van would work for that plan B. It was covered, could carry them all, and it was extra. Although it provided an effective roadblock at the front of the 500-foot driveway, it attracted unwanted attention. Another gate at the front of the drive was necessary. Maybe a telephone pole on a hinge?

After telling Tim and Philip his plan, Jason grabbed the van keys and drove it down the blacktop, cutting off on the gravel road heading for Robert's house. Turning right after about ¼ mile, Jason doubled back on the edge of the field to its shaded corner by the creek, right behind his house. The van did not seem visible from any road. *If* the dirt trail remained passable, (a *big* if) the van might provide a means for Jason's family to escape. A trail across the creek, or maybe a bridge, was in order as time permitted. Jason made his way down one bank and up the other. Sure enough, it was steep and the thorns made it nearly impassable. So much to do.

It was almost dark. Jason had heard the chainsaw and did not know why. When he walked up the back pasture, he could see Tim and Phil falling a light pole next to the shed. The glass shattered and the cable lay on the ground.

"That wire is still live, by the way. I got this nylon cord and I am going to string it up to that oak and lift up that wire."

"Do we still have power?"

"Umm." Tim grinned sheepishly. "I don't know. Hang on. Haley!"

They still had power, and Tim did what he said. It wasn't up to Stone Electric standards no doubt, but it was taped off well and up out of harm's way. Philip dragged it, broken light and all, down to the front of the driveway, with Jason and Tim tagging behind.

"It can lay there tonight," Jason remarked. "We can drill and hinge something for it tomorrow maybe. We have plenty of posts, but I am thinking those cross ties should be heavy enough if we can rig up some cable support." There was little light left. The sun had set, sudden and dark, due to clouds in the west, which meant possible rain.

When people work, people eat. Food was on the table when Jason, Peter, and Philip came inside. Haley and Tim were back on sentry. The two hours every night keeping watch was taking its toll on all of them. Everyone had talked about maybe only having one sentry at night. It might be a good idea, yet it might get them killed. Who knew?

Deborah had found some of Jason's old battle dress uniforms, which fit both Phil and Peter well. Jason had taken to wearing his ACU uniform for the last couple of days, while Tim wore mechanic overalls. Military uniforms could withstand a lot.

Plans were made as to where the extra firing positions would be, if an emergency called for it. If any sentry signaled or fired, the entire family was to help defend. If it looked like it was an overwhelming force, the family would bug out across the creek to the van and take off. It was the front sentry's job to hold off a frontal assault until the family was in the van. Then, with help of the second sentry, both guards were to retreat with covering fire, across the creek to bug out. If that were not possible, the front sentry would hold off the force as long as possible providing frontal then flanking fire while under concealment of the woods, and withdraw through the woods, moving to the established rally point within 12 hours. All good on paper, but the plan needed practice.

That evening, Jason turned on the television to watch the bad news. On a national level, the United States had defaulted on its debts and caused what appeared to be a global economic meltdown. The stock market in Hong Kong, the only one still open, reported record losses. In the Pacific, there was a tense standoff between China and the United States. South Korea and Japan were being remarkably silent about the situation, perhaps reckoning that it was better to remain neutral. No conflict had yet taken place, but there was talk of Chinese cruise missiles potentially attacking the Pacific fleet poised 250 miles southeast of Hong Kong, and possible retaliation from U.S. Navy submarines.

Local news was little better. About 70 miles away, Memphis, Tennessee was being destroyed by violent clashes between local residents and anyone else foolish enough to be found in that city. All local Memphis television stations were off the air. KAET, the local news station, reported rolling electrical blackouts in the region. That day, while Jason was at the Everling farm, they had lost power for 20 minutes. Most businesses in the surrounding towns were closed. At the Middleton Wal-Mart, which had hired private security, a robbery had taken place and five people had been killed, including an 8-year-old girl. The governor of Arkansas had declared an emergency for the entire state, imposing marshal law. A curfew of 6:00 p.m. was in effect. That was enough television for one night.

Although the living room was the TV room, at least as long as there was to be electricity, it was also turning into the mecca for board games. It seemed there were some advantages to having six people in one place. For the next two hours, Jason and Peter thoroughly enjoyed having their rear ends handed to them on a platter in a game of Mexican Dominoes. Deborah won, with a bragging Philip a close second.

Then it was Jason's time on sentry: 10:00 p.m. A quiet time. The clouded night partially veiled the small round moon. The family dog, Bailey, seldom barked. When she did, it was normally because a rabbit or coyote was around. Now, however, the friendly boxer lay in her bed under the carport. Rounding the corner of the house, Jason whistled lightly, then approached Tim at the sentry post, avoiding the gravel of the drive itself. Noise discipline. Tim, properly relieved, walked back the same way after commenting on how quiet it had been. Deborah had walked to her own post by the split oak, carrying the 12 gauge. Although it was too dark to see her in the shadows, he knew she was there, and that thought made him somehow happy. Later on, he would walk over and say hi. Not now though. He had to get his night vision. He had grown accustomed to the sounds of night. The crickets chirped their song, their chant slowed by the chilly air, to the accompaniment of the frogs from the two nearby ponds. A vehicle was in the distance, there were fewer and fewer vehicles that went down the narrow blacktop ribbon that cut through the hills in front of their house. It did not pass by, no doubt having turned in somewhere. Pushing himself against the trunk of the large oak, he placed his SKS on his lap and listened. He heard the bay of a dog, a beagle perhaps, which had been startled. Now that was the kind of dog Jason needed. Maybe two or three of them, placed in the bottomland behind the pond. A dog like that would wake the dead. Perhaps a German Shepherd also for the front yard. With sentry duty, there was always time to think.

After a while, Jason walked down the drive in the shadow of the trees to where they had dragged the light pole that day. Across the road, lights were on in the distance. Jason had not realized how much of an advertisement to would-be criminals those lights served at night. Although it had been simply a consequence of necessity, Jason was glad that the mercury vapor light pole was gone.

Quietly, Jason made his way back up the hill, his rifle at port, and walked back to his post. He had called his mother today. She was with his step-dad in Mississippi. Although his mother was 70, she carried a .357 revolver, which she had named Bessie, with her everywhere. Mr. Ron was taking care of her the best he could. Their neighborhood had formed a watch program, which manned roadblocks on the county road to their house. Mr. Ron was there now, pulling an all-night shift. Their neighbor across the street, a widow twenty years her younger, was staying with them at their house. His mom and her husband were safe. He wondered how long the cell service would last. Cellphones would be missed.

He pulled out his phone and texted his wife, telling her he was coming over. Getting mistakenly shot by your wife would be bad, Jason mused as he slung his weapon across his back and made his way across the yard. Ironically, although they had been together for the last 4 days, Jason and Deborah hadn't really had any time together. She stood as he walked toward her, a glimpse of moonlight making its way through the clouds to catch her hair, making her shine. He walked behind her and held her, placing his mouth against her neck. Somehow holding her made everything better, made the madness of the last few days go away. They held hands and walked in the shadows, mindful of their watch but also of their need to be together. Rule one of survival: Have someone worth living for. He had found that someone.

The entire house was black as they held hands and walked in the dimly lit yard. Canvas, taken from a General Purpose military tent, which Jason had years earlier purchased on a whim, had been used to provide effective blackout curtains for all the house's windows and doors. As it was, at night the entire house was invisible from the edge of the yard, and most certainly, from the road. Indeed, the entire front of their split-level home was unoccupied that night to help with both noise and light discipline. Therefore, it was a certainty that no one saw Jason and Deborah holding each other, forgetting all the chaos around them, and kissing in the moonlight.

4 MARAUDERS

Some people believe in chance, or luck, a belief that happenstance and misfortune falls upon anyone. Jason was not such a person. He believed in providence, and preparation. Perhaps it was providence that his family did not fall victim to the band of looters. The electric had gone out that next morning, but Jason had been listening to the battery-powered radio. There he had heard the report that several truckloads of looters were systematically ransacking houses along Highway 167. What little law enforcement that remained in the local area was simply too undermanned. Many police officers had simply quit, choosing instead to protect their own families.

The whole world has gone crazy, Jason thought. Jason walked down to the highway, and out of habit, checked the mail. Nothing, of course. He noticed neighbors in the two houses across the street packing up their vehicles. Jason said hello and walked up to his closest neighbor. He did not know them very well, but they seemed like a nice couple. They had knocked at the door one time telling him that his dog had run loose.

"Haven't you heard. There was a big prisoner escape at the county jail. They are coming down the ridge this way. We are going south to stay at her uncle's." The man's wife closed the door to their trailer carrying a laundry basket of food.

"Look, what if we just stayed together. You two could come over. We could try to protect ourselves," Jason offered.

"You ain't listening. There are a bunch of them. With guns. The police don't even answer when you call." The man closed the hatch of his suburban. "If you was smart, you would leave, too." The man closed the SUV's door, and sped away, spinning the tires a bit on the gravel drive.

The other neighbor, a single mother of two teens, had a similar story. Her weathered face witnessed that she had already lived a hard life. "We are going to Middleton. The government has food and shelters set up there.

"But you could stay with us."

The neighbor looked at him, a bit impatient to get on the road. "Look, that's what the government is for. You need to leave yourself."

Jason walked up the long drive back to the house. It might take a while before the band of marauders made it this far. They were about 10 miles away and headed south. They had more than enough time to...leave? There was absolutely no way that his family would be able to defend against such animals. Not right now. His family had neither the weapons nor the manpower to defend against such a mob. Yet if his family ran, they would be exposed, without food, water, or security. Jason doubted if the government would take care of his family. The police could not even respond to emergencies, much less an armed mob. No, Jason needed a plan.

That morning Jason had his family place some food and blankets in the van parked across the creek. The bulk of the essential supplies however; food, clothing, medicine, and the like; were placed in the storm shelter next to the house. The emergency shelter had never been used, yet now seemed like a befitting time. Jason and Philip removed the vents, capping them off. Within two hours, Tim had loaded his dump truck and covered the storm shelter and the propane tank next to it in a mound of dirt 5 feet tall. Phil and Peter took canvas with them into the adjacent woods about 10 yards in. Being careful to not disturb the screening vegetation, they placed the canvas sheets on the ground and covered them with leaves. The plan was simple: make their house the most inviting. Inside the house, individual bottles of alcohol were set out: Jason's entire supply of rum, whiskey, and vodka was placed in open view. Pillows, blankets, and mattresses, were all brought down to the living room. Even a stash of Hustler magazines, which Jason had found in the white van, were scattered out in the living room. The grill was made ready. All to welcome their new guests. With all the preparations, nightfall came quickly.

"Guys," Jason had explained. "There is no way we can take these guys in an all-out fight. But out on the road, we are exposed, vulnerable." Jason, let them ponder this for a moment.

"This is our home. We cannot let these criminals take what is ours. Now we must be patient." That evening, the family waited under the tarps at the edge of the woods. All night. The next morning, there was quiet discussion about leaving. Bathroom breaks were taken. A box of Ritz crackers was passed around. Should they simply get in the van and take off now? Where would they go?

It was noon when Peter saw the smoke, and about three hours later when they heard their blood-lust cries coming down the road. Gunfire from across the road. A woman's scream, which seemed to continue for eternity before it stopped. Some neighbor had chosen to stay. Jason, who had second-guessed his decision to stay all evening, was now thinking he should have escaped with his family in the van, but it was too late.

Three vehicles then pulled up their driveway, which was not blocked, not locked; all was open. Even the door to the house was unlocked for Jason had removed the doorknobs. A crash, and then a joyous cry was heard inside the house as Jason's family lay under the camouflaged canvas. Music from the family's three battery powered radios was blaring, and shots were fired in the air as the marauders celebrated their new found paradise. The smell of cooking meat filled the air. The home invaders had evidently found one of Jason's sheep. Jason's family waited, hiding under the canvas. Then came shrill screams. At first, incessant cries for help, then begging and moaning amidst drunken laughter. On and on. Throughout the evening. It was torment for the family to listen to the agony just a few yards away in their own home. Apparently, the bastards had brought what they considered entertainment. Jason whispered to the family, "When our time comes, we will show *them* no mercy. Do you understand?" Tim, Philip, and Peter answered. Deborah and Haley simply nodded quietly.

It was light, but just barely. There was a morning mist when four men and two women crept from the canvas. Rifles and shotguns in hand, pistols in their belts, the military-clad family took their positions. Jason with SKS in hand and Philip, carrying his 12 gauge, crawled toward the front door of their violated home. With its security door removed and the hinges well oiled, the door opened noiselessly.

Out back, Deborah waited behind the cover of a vehicle, placing the barrel of her deer rifle into the open window of a 2014 Dodge Ram pickup. Its muzzle was directed at the temple of a huge fellow, a drunken, sleeping brute of a man who had fallen asleep in the driver's seat. His drawers were dropped; he apparently had passed out reading the August 2013 edition of Hustler magazine.

Tim made his way through the side door of the house with a 12 gauge, while Haley and Peter covered the carport from around the side of the house with another kind of weapon, Molotov cocktails. All faces were stoic. They knew what must happen to these evil men.

Upstairs appeared empty. It seemed all had availed themselves of the party room prepared for them. Jason was not feeling polite enough to knock before entering the living room below.

Bursting in the living room, Jason emptied his SKS within 10 seconds, the sound of the assault rifle deafening in the large room. The smell of sex, smoke, and alcohol mixed with that of gunpowder as Tim began firing in the living room from the side door. Half naked men, totally unarmed, were defenseless against the hail of bullets and buckshot. Behind his father, who was pumping lead from his Browning 9mm into the room below, Philip stood rear guard shotgun at ready. Suddenly an overweight black man came at him, charging across the dining room from the master bedroom. Phillip greeted the unwelcome guest with buckshot. Instantly pumping another round, Philip fired a slug into the thigh of a second marauder, a person so tall, he must have played professional sports. Unfortunately for the man, this was not basketball. The tall would-be aggressor went down immediately in agonizing pain. Philip rushed into the master bedroom, emptying his shotgun, and then pulled out a 9mm semiautomatic, firing with both hands. Five people rushed out the back door of the bedroom, to where Haley and Peter waited with fire. Flaming bottles broke on the brick steps, engulfing the escaping men in flames.

In the living room, Tim and Jason were death angels. Two men, still in a half-drunken stupor, managed to find the door. Deborah, waiting for them outside, missed the first man, but shot the second man in the chest. Peter and Haley, who were peppering the five burning men with .22 rounds, turned their attention to the one escaping man who was getting away. He had run around the house. Deborah bolted another round, sighted in the .308, and, squeezed. She did not miss that second time. Jason, who was busy dealing death in the living room, bayoneted a man who was missing most of his intestines, and then turned to another man who was getting up to aim a revolver. Jason drove the bayonet forward toward the man's face. 18" of steel was the last that entered the drunken attacker's mind. Jason allowed his rifle to tilt under the weight of the suddenly limp, lifeless body, shoving the dead man clear with his boot. There was an eerie, surreal silence. Jason, pumped full of adrenaline, was looking from side to side, taken aback by the slaughter.

Recovering, Jason let out a piercing whistle. Peter and Haley ran to the front yard to keep watch behind the old oak. Jason shouted out the back door: "We are coming out." Deborah was still holding the deer rifle, supporting her aim using the truck. Then, the reality hit her. In front of her, in the cab of the truck, lay a huge brute of a man, missing half of his head. She had killed three men. Still holding her rifle at ready, she vomited on the hood of the vehicle.

After checking on his wife, Jason, Tim, and Philip made a sweep of the house. It was inside the master bedroom, they found the two dead teenage girls who had been tied with baling wire. They both apparently had bled to death. It was not a pleasant sight.

Both Haley and Peter had made it to the front gate through sheer adrenaline, but were now both weeping. The front yard turned into a gathering place. There the shocked and sickened family took turns crying, holding each other, ...and reloading.

About 20 minutes after the slaughter, a vehicle pulled in the drive, a police cruiser. Peter was the first to stand, his .22 raised, then Jason and

Deborah, then the others. It was the policeman who had come the week before, Officer Henry. Inside his cruiser were his wife and teenage son. They needed a place to stay.

Death is not some movie scene. People see dead animals on the side of the road and avert their eyes. People smile and visit at funerals, never directly addressing what has brought them together. Death leaves an ugly scar. It was over a week before any of Jason's family could sleep in their house. They slept in the shed. Deborah would cry hysterically over small things, such as when she found that one of her porcelain plates broke. Peter did not speak for a week. No one slept well for some time afterwards. That day there had been thirteen dead bodies at the Hamilton residence. But none were the bodies of Jason's family.

* * *

Shock and Recovery

It was Officer Henry and his wife, Margarita, that had made the difference during that time. The first week was quiet, and so was the family. Jason, Philip, and Tim buried the two teenage girls in the back pasture. The rest were loaded in the dump truck, and disposed of in an open field 4 miles away, soaked with diesel, and burned. Blood came off through with scrubbing, carpets were torn up, and bullet holes were patched inside. Luckily, the Molotov cocktails thrown had hit brick and wet grass or there would not have been a house to clean. Jason swore to himself that he would never let this happen to his family, to his home, again.

Margarita cooked for everyone. Margarita's refried beans, tortillas, and rice as well as her easy laughter brought life back to the family. She was good company for Deborah and Haley. Watching their son Edwardo interact with Peter was medicinal, and it brought Jason's son back from his traumatic shell-shock. Eventually Deborah, Haley, and Peter, indeed they all, were able to recover from the nightmare they had experienced.

It was a full seven days afterward before Jason had the drive to wonder what had become of his neighbors. What he found was devastating.

The neighbors down the road had been killed: their bodies bloated and half-eaten in the yard, their trailer burned. Jason, Officer Henry, and Tim resigned themselves to funeral detail, disposing of their remains in the dump truck. Down Deer Run Road, much the same. Some houses had been apparently untouched. Others had been looted. Five more dead at the Gosling residence across from Bo's place. A young man, (Had Jason not taught him in school?) his mother, father, sister, and some other girl had chosen to make their stand as well. Four of them had been shot outright. The young girl apparently had not been so lucky. Her eyes staring lifeless, her heavy ruined mascara emphatic of the misery she had suffered. Tim placed a blanket over her naked and abused body. Most of the neighbors had left. The last house on Deer Run Road, a house a half-mile farther down, hidden by trees, had been protected. A rather large tree had fallen, effectively blocking the road. Upon closer examination, however, the tree looked to have been sawed down. Traveling the rest of road on foot, they came to the home's gate. Jason's party was expected.

"That's far enough."

"I am Jason Hamilton, your neighbor. I live at 18210 Highway 167. We survived, too. We have food, supplies, and some medicine. We only want to help." To verify his story, he recounted meeting the man's wife, who had volunteered at a local election.

The man lowered his rifle, what appeared to be a .270 Remington. "My son has been shot in the leg. He has an infection."

"We have ampicillin and pain meds at home. Plus, my wife has medical training. We can provide security if you want to take him there."

"My wife and I heard about those sons-of-bitches coming. Most everyone else ran off. I felled the tree across the road back there. I guess they never realized we were out here." Indeed, no one would have ever suspected a house so far deep in the woods down a dead end road.

"If you want, we can help you take him to our place. You can follow us out."

While driving back, Jason rode shotgun with Jeb Walker and his wife Nora in their Lincoln Towncar back to the fallen tree. Although Philip and Tim had insisted on walking, Jeb was yet more adamant that they ride "rumble seat" sitting on the open trunk. Within a moment of arriving at the roadblock, the dump truck was brought to life and the tree had been pulled from the road. "That was Jeb's idea," Nora pointed to the dead end road sign immediately ahead. Jeb had actually made the road seem unused, having placed three small shrubs in the road and what looked like bags of leaves and debris scattered on the roadway. From a distance, the road indeed had looked like an abandoned trail.

Arriving back home, the injured youth was brought inside. Deborah had never worked a gunshot wound before. Two weeks ago, her daughter had downloaded medical files from the web. Using an electric converter, the laptop was brought to life. Inside one file, there was a picture of a gunshot wound and instructions. In the picture, the entrance wound looked as though it could be stitched easily, but the exit wound looked like a mushroom of pink shredded meat. The young man's wound, however, looked different. Apparently Nora had dressed the entrance wound well. The young man's calf looked as if it were healing, despite the bruising around the hole. The exit wound was another story. The shredded tissue had been cut away, and the resulting wound was still somewhat open. It was seeping clear fluid, but pus was beginning to form. There was a reddish tint around the exit wound. Infection had set in. In the days before penicillin, this young man would have definitely lost his leg. Even now, he still might. "I have never done this before," Deborah confided to Jeb and Nora what Jason already knew.

"Just help him if you can."

"I am going to sterilize, make some small incisions, treat it again with antibiotic ointment. It looks like you have already done that."

"I worked in a veterinarian's clinic for 8 years."

"Then you have more experience than me, Nora," Deborah chuckled lightly. "Let's get that done, and afterwards we can give him more ampicillin. We will keep his wound clean and hope for the best."

It was Deborah's heart to help others that kept Jason falling in love with her every day. Jason realized if he were only trying to survive to save himself, he was little different than those animals that had invaded their home.

That night Jason yet again struggled to sleep. Had he done wrong? Could he have saved others in the community? Harold's words came back to him. "Help your sons. Trust no one else." Yet surely there had to be a compromise. He could help others and still protect his family, right? Jason studied his actions of the previous week. He had had no choice. He had done the right thing. Jason would help others in the community, if possible. In some ways, building a network might be a better way to defend his family. But Jason's family came first.

* * *

Living without electricity brought its own sets of problems. One small but notable thing was that everyone suffered from electronic device withdrawal. Unlike power outages in the past, Jason was unable to go to the store for extra batteries, fuel, fast food, and a simple escape. For everyday use, flashlights were slowly replaced by hurricane lamps, barn lamps, candles, and, of course, windows. Reading became a popular hobby, and Jason found himself wishing he had more of a collection. As it was, every family member except for Tim would read Fifty Shades of Grey that first year. Tim would hold out on sheer principle. Jason himself took to writing a journal.

Cooking and heating became more of a chore without electricity. The microwave, refrigerator, and stove had been reduced to nothing more than pantry areas for jars and cans. Simply cooking a meal took more time without the electric stove or microwave. Larger pots were scrounged to prepare more food for more people. The Dutch Ovens and iron skillets were especially helpful as they could hold heat longer without burning food. Since the refrigerator did not work, ice chests held leftovers, and as the weather got colder, so did the storm shelter. The colder weather made Jason appreciate the Peacock stove, used for both cooking and heating in the living room. It became evident, however, that the family would need another wood stove upstairs if the cold were to be bearable this winter.

It was Margarita who was a Godsend. She kept up a friendly chat while she worked. "I always make three cups of beans per person and three cups rice." "Meat goes bad quick so keep it on hoof." or "Oh, girl, did you know you can grind rice to make flour? I watched my mother do this as a girl." Evidently she had been raised in Mexico in a home with a wood stove and limited resources. "I still member how to do these things," Margarita told Deborah and Haley. Then she smiled broadly and laughed. "I was just hoping I would not need to remember them anymore." Deborah just had to smile back at the way she said "Remeamber."

After one week without power, there was no running water. The toilets still could be flushed since Jason's place had a septic system. It was the "You use the bucket; you fill the bucket" honor system. Rain barrels were placed under each house gutter to collect water for purposes such as that. Jason did have a water well down by the shed, but it required hand-pumping. Tim had been studying on the running water issue as well, saying if they could get a pump and pressure tank, perhaps he could power it with a generator. A gasoline pump would be more efficient on gas, he stated, but finding one with right specs might be difficult. "Lowe's should have one." Tim gave that sheepish grin that always followed his jokes.

No hot water had been a major issue for Jason. Before the Tuesday Meltdown, poor hygiene had been considered a personal issue, but it was becoming more and more a health issue since the power outage. Jason was still reminded of the British sergeant major with whom he had served. The sergeant major had inspected the hands of every soldier in his unit before every mealtime. "Clean those nails," he would tell a soldier, then slap him in the face. Dysentery, Jason recalled, was the number one health concern in many countries. Tim's ingenuity, however, had quickly solved the hot water problem. Tim had taken a 55-gallon barrel and soldered a water nozzle to the side. The barrel was placed over an outdoor fireplace constructed out of bricks and blocks. A simple water hose was screwed into the nozzle. "Won't the hose burn?" Jason asked. Tim smiled and replied matter-of-factly, "I will let you know when I find out."

5 NEW NEIGHBORS

    Tim didn't realize it, but part of Jason did not take going shopping as a joke. Of all the preparations Jason had made for possible emergencies, he had not prepared well enough to take in nine people. Jason needed to find food. What about blankets? Another wood stove? After all, the propane would not last forever. Hand tools were another issue. Just how many hand tools did Jason have? Sure a power saw could operate on a generator and a chain saw on gas. But just how long would their fuel hold out? Coffee would be nice to have again, or maybe a percolator that made more than four cups at a time. Shopping wasn't such a bad idea, but going to Middleton did not seem like such a safe option. Keeping a low profile seemed important. Jason recalled the reaction at Wal-Mart again. The way things were now, people were probably killing for food in town.

    Guns and ammunition were the one thing that did not seem to be in short supply, thanks to their recently deceased home invaders. There were two dozen firearms among the dead, in their vehicles: pistols and rifles of both hunting and military specs. Jason eyed the inventory, now placed against the front wall of their dining room, cleaned and loaded: among the various pistols, most 9mm, .45 caliber semis, and revolvers, stood four 5.56 caliber AR 15s, four scoped hunting rifles, and two 9mm carbines. Ammunition supplies were incredible. 3,000 rounds of 9mm Luger ammunition (if Philip counted right) and 500 rounds of 9mm jacketed hollow points. A similar amount of the .223. Boxes upon boxes of 12 and 20 gauge shells, sabot rounds, slugs, buckshot, and even game load and bird shot. It was as if the marauders had cleaned out a major sporting goods store with plans to go to war. Jason, however was not worried about going to war; he had to feed, clothe, and house his family. Jason needed supplies.

The only alternative to going to town for supplies would be to scavenge from other homes. It might seem frivolous for a person who had taken so many lives to worry about taking possessions from abandoned homes. It was, however, the principle of the matter. A man's home was his castle, and his possessions, his own. Anyone who violated that precept deserved to be shot. Jason needed to think. A walk might do him good. A walk might help Jason think.

The fourteen acres on the south side of Jason's property had been termed "the woods." It loosely qualified, mostly secondary growth with a few tall pines, oaks, and gum trees. It was thick with undergrowth although narrow paths had been made for contingency evasion plans. Jason chose instead to make his way through the brush. A verse from Wordsworth, the road not taken entered his mind: "But knowing how way leads on to way, I doubted if I should ever come back." Indeed his path had made a different turn. Jason did not walk, nor did he creep. He moved carefully, deliberately, through the thicket. Not a sound. Moving this way demanded attention and energy. It was a discipline that his mind needed. The damp leaves made little noise as he placed one foot down and moved slowly ahead. His jacket and slow deliberate movements kept the thorns from catching him. The entire time Jason looked around, for movement, for animals. A sparrow was directly in front of him about 10 feet, but was never startled as Jason slowly moved on. A mockingbird dropped a feather to his right. Still moving on. He was in no hurry, but was patiently making his way. To protect his family required patience as well. It had not been necessary to scavenge others homes before now. There had been enough. But more food was needed for winter now. On the other side of the pond ahead of him were two ducks, a drake and his mate. Jason slowly raised his rifle and sighted in on the drake...No, there might be time for hunting, later. He lowered his rifle. There was work to be done.

"With this winter coming, we are going to need supplies. More hay for the animals. Also, there may be others needing our help in the local area. We need to continue looking for survivors in this neighborhood. If there is anything that can be used from a house that has been abandoned, we take it." Officer Henry began making a list. Livestock, canned goods, animal feed, hay, plastic and tarp materials, wood stoves, large pots, anything that could store water or be used as a fuel container, fuels...the list grew quite long.

There were 9 of them. Six of them would go out. Trees would be fallen at the bridges at Big Creek and Church Creek, each about 1/2 mile distant from the Hamilton's drive. A vehicle would be parked on each bridge. Jason had halved the distance in his mind, then mapped it out. A lookout with a hunting rifle would wait in hiding about 400 yards from the bridge. "It will have to be 500 yards on the south side by Big Creek, that way you can be concealed from the edge of the woods. Highway 167 is the only road in and out of here, and we can keep this neighborhood reasonably secure." The third person was to remain on the hill at Bo's place as backup. One shot and the group would converge at the front driveway.

    The salvage team was divided into 3 teams: Jason and Deborah on food detail, Officer Henry and Margarita on materials, anything from stoves and generators, to blankets, and Tim with Haley on fuel detail, which consisted of driving vehicles to the house, draining vehicle tanks, and looking for propane. Peter, Philip, and Edwardo were on watch. Jeb kindly agreed to stand watch with Peter on Bo's Hill, while Nora stayed at the Hamilton home with her injured son, whose fever was breaking.

    It seems that that the marauders who had visited this neighborhood were more set upon general murder and mayhem than looting. Empty houses remained relatively unscathed. Other houses had been emptied of food, their owners having fled in fear of their lives. Still these houses were a virtual treasure trove for the teams. In the front yard of one house were two iron cook pots, hanging on hoops. One was cracked, but the other was intact. Once outdated relics, now with situations changed, these iron pots were an efficient way to heat wash water. Sheets and blankets were packed in the Dodge Ram's roomy bed, along with spare pairs of boots, and assorted ponchos, jackets, and mud-waders. The truck's bed became piled-over as oil lamps, candles, a wood splitter, axes, shovels, even a two-man crosscut saw were found.

    "Peter and Philip are going to love this," Jason smiled at the thought.

    One lesson learned early on was not to open up freezers. Although it had been less than two weeks since the power had been lost, an incredibly powerful odor of rot and death was developing.

    Tim and Haley had found a dozen gas cans, most of them empty. In addition, they had discovered about a dozen 20 gallon propane tanks and one larger 100 gallon tank. Four vehicles had been found which seemed near full of gas, and they had been transported back home. Tim remarked to Jason about the situation: "We need a couple of large fuel tanks, to be honest with you. One for gas and one for diesel. That way we can pump or siphon fuel, then store it."

    It was getting late when Tim started up a diesel engine in the back of one of the farmhouses. A 40 HP John Deere tractor, complete with front-end loader, and something on the back. As Tim revved up the engine and rounded the front of the white wood-framed house, Jason noticed what was mounted on the back. Something that would prove to be invaluable that next spring: a disk plow.

    At the end of the day, Officer Henry and Margarita came back with their load of medical supplies and tools. Circular saws, chain saws, drills, and hand tools were in the back of a weathered blue F250, which Henry thought more appropriate than the cruiser for scavenging. In addition, several cardboard boxes of gauze, iodine, alcohol, along with penicillin, insulin, and pain medications were found. Although none of the crew smoked, and drinking wasn't a big pastime recently, Henry and Margarita had nevertheless brought back quite a few cartons of cigarettes and bottles of hard liquor. "Good trading material," Jason agreed.

The biggest surprise was found in the dog pens. Two short-haired terriers and a German Shepherd. "We couldn't leave em," Henry commented. "Another two dogs were already dead. No water, and they hadn't eaten. The German Shepherd was in the house at the end of Weldon's Run. He had torn up the house trying to find food. Thought I would have to shoot him at first. I shut the door, then came back with dog food. He is a good dog."

That night, after a meal prepared from canned goods, Jason and Officer Henry had a talk. "Well it is a bit crowded," Henry said.

"It is up to you. And you never know if or when Bo will be coming back," Jason said.

"Look, that property is a big problem. It is unoccupied. And honestly, we do need space," Officer Henry responded.

"I don't like the way you can see it from the road."

"With the extended parameters we are monitoring now, we have enough warning."

Jason understood the advantages of everyone staying together, but he also understood the necessity of being independent, to work for one's self. Indeed the first permanent American settlement at Jamestown was almost destroyed due to its flawed design of collective living. A person should work with his own hands.

So it was discussed and agreed upon. The Henry's would stay at Bo Henderson's residence. The residence was close enough to maintain a united defense. Henry had plans to place a barbed wire fence along the front of the yard.

"I have been thinking about barbed wire some," Jason commented. "Our fence is already 5 strands, wired for cattle. I was thinking about driving another set of metal fence poles at a 45-degree angle with three strands of barbed wire. It would make the fence much more difficult to cross."

"What should happen to those two fire trucks?" Bo's son had had an unusual habit, restoring fire engines. The two bright red trucks, indeed the entire place, had not been bothered during the brigand raid the week before.

"You know, I had thought those two fire trucks next door would make a good barrier. But now I'm second-guessing myself. Who knows if or when we might need the use of a fire engine, especially with those pumps?"

And so it was that the Henry family moved next door. A pact was made that both families would hold a common defense, manning Bo Hill with two lookouts. Jeb, Nora, and Jackson also agreed to maintain the lookouts, although they lived almost mile away down Deer Run Road. "It is the only real way into the neighborhood, except for through the woods. So we benefit as well. We should contribute," Jeb explained.

News had become increasingly bad since what had been termed "The Tuesday Meltdown." (Thank God for radio, which remained on the air.) The federal government had mandated that major grocery stores and department stores remain open. No one, however, could mandate that employees come to work at those stores. The result was state and local government employees working grocery detail while the Arkansas National Guard were tasked to provide security. There was a limited supply of food both at Kroger and Wal-Mart Supercenter. You could get some basic food items there, but there was a catch: you must apply for the Supplemental Nutrition Assistance Program, or SNAP as it was called. You must apply, hat-in-hand, for welfare.

Security in the Kroger parking lot was sufficient to protect citizens while there. When people left the parking lot, however, was another story. Where marshal law prohibited law-abiding citizens from carrying guns in the city, the declaration was not observed by the lawless, who carried out daylight car-jackings and robberies at major intersections without much threat of reprisal from law enforcement and National Guardsmen, who were stretched thin.

There was talk of a federal law being passed making it mandatory for everyone to apply for the SNAP program. Ben Decker, a national radio talk show host, who was still on-the-air somewhere in Utah, was broadcasting information that apparently the federal government did not want to publish. Mr. Decker had had a warrant for his arrest in the state of New York, and now had a federal warrant. His crime...federal tax evasion. Even now, the IRS was hunting him.

"...which is why Washington wants you to sign up for SNAP. With Executive Order 13603 and how it relates to SNAP, the federal government can search your home without warrant or probable cause. It can confiscate your home if you are found hoarding food or found with an assault-style firearm within your home. You might ask, 'Who gets to define hoarding?' The Department of Homeland Security on-site commander. Talk about the fox guarding the hen house."

As Ben Decker continued his evening broadcast, the A.M. signal began to drift and fade. The information he had brought, however, remained firmly in the family's mind.

"I know one thing. I am never going to give up my right to protect my family," Jason announced. The idea that the government had already routinely violated almost every amendment in the Bill of Rights left Jason, Officer Henry, and Jeb worried. Would they be considered criminals simply because they were protecting their families and providing for themselves?

*　*　*

Visitors

It was then that they all were startled by a gunshot. Philip, Peter, and Edwardo, who were manning sentry at Bo Hill, had seen something. Immediately, the families rushed to throw on boots, grabbing rifles and ammo belts as they ran out the door. Within 5 minutes, the sentries had the support of 9 heavily armed and well-positioned fighters. Even in the rush of the moment, Jason managed to see the improvement in their security, while still realizing its inadequacy.

"Dad, that sign is large enough to read it easily. I know they saw it. They had a flashlight on," Phillip whispered. Indeed, the sign had been large enough. Posted at both Big Creek and Church Creek barricades, 4' x 8' signs stated:

> "The people living here are peaceful. We seek no trouble and desire to be left in peace. If you wish to talk, have one person walk up the highway unarmed with his hands up. If not, you will all be killed." [It was Philip's idea to post the smiley face and "Have a nice day!" at the bottom.]

The night was dark and quiet. Clouds covered the rising moon and very few stars were visible. Before the meltdown, few people had any idea of how dark the night could be. This particular night was a blanket of darkness. No vehicle lights had been seen approaching. And since Philip's shot, no noise. It was nerve-wracking.

"What should we do?" Officer Henry had asked. He and his family had been busy relocating earlier that evening. Indeed both families had been transporting food, clothes, ammunition, arms, and other items the 600 feet or so from Jason's storage building to what would be now termed the Henry residence.

"We stay. We listen. It is too dark out there tonight," Jason replied. Noisemakers, actually little more than cans with pea gravel, had been wired up along the northern and southern bounds of "Bo Hill" for almost a quarter mile in each direction. Deer and dogs made for many false alarms during the dark of night, but tonight they might prove their worth. About 400 feet from each bridge, Edwardo and Peter had been manning observation posts. Edwardo, on the northern perimeter had seen something and had diligently called it in on his walkie-talkie. Although the two-way radios were actually child toys, even having Scooby Doo characters stamped on the front, the 9-volt battery-powered devices still functioned well. Since the loss of cellphone service, they had been invaluable.

All night the families waited. About 3 a.m. the coyotes cried and dogs sounded a return. A heavy mist formed about 4:30 a.m, completely obscuring the barricade a ¼ mile away. The autumn nights had been getting longer, as summer had grown to a distant memory. It was getting colder. In the early morning, a defiant red rooster had started crowing back at the Hamilton residence. Somewhere in the distance, a dog barked. One of Jason's terriers sounded off a quick bay in return. An hour passed. It was about 7:00 a.m. when the sun began to peak over the horizon.

Deborah, Margarita, and Nora were bringing out coffee and biscuits while the bleary-eyed men discussed what exactly should be done. Under the idea that the best defense was a good offense, the men agreed that four of them would form a scrimmage line through the trees along the ridge, searching the west side of the highway. If contact was made, perhaps there could be discussions. If hostile action was encountered, however, it would be met with deadly force.

Warmed with coffee and biscuits, the four men aligned 10 yards apart and started walking quietly in unison, maintaining an overwatch line as they passed the two untouched homes across from the Henry residence. It was a shame that those houses were not inhabited, Jason thought as he walked the line's right flank immediately behind the homes.

Passing through the woods, the men carried the same slow, deliberate pace. Jason carried the 9mm carbine at low port. Where most people had discounted the 9mm Hi-point carbine as a cheap firearm, Jason had found that the Hi-point 995 was very reliable with feeding, due to its direct blow-back cycle. Supposedly it could be fired covered in mud, making it as reliable as his trusted SKS. Jason liked the solid feel of the weapon. At his side, he carried his Browning 9mm pistol. Although definitely not a Glock, the Browning nevertheless had been standard issue for many military and law enforcement institutions around the globe. It also happened to be Jason's sidearm of choice.

The woods behind the Lighthouse Pentecostal Church had been cleared recently, making the movement quieter. Church Creek lay directly in front of them, presenting a challenge. Should they go around and walk on the highway? No, if so, any element of surprise would be lost. They would cross here. Jason was the first to transverse the creek, grasping kudzu vines to balance him. As he moved across the creek, the cold, knee-deep water filled his tan military boots, weighing him down a bit as he climbed the far bank. Taking position next to a tree behind the white wooden church, he signaled Jeb and Henry to follow. Finally, Henry stayed to help Tim up the creek's bank as dawn broke over the empty fields to their east.

High crawling past the windows, Jason and Henry moved to the front door with Tim behind them. Henry counted down on his fingers, and Jason moved in first, carbine ready, with Henry following. Up front, on a small raised stage behind the plain wooden pulpit, a Mexican woman looked at him with wide eyes. Something familiar about her, Jason thought. The woman cried out "Juan" and another frightened face, bruised and cut, appeared. Jason recognized the Mexican man he had given a ride a few weeks back.

Walking back to the barricade, Juan and his wife Gabrielle explained in their limited English how they had been driven from their home. "They say we no belong here," Juan said. His face looked painful, with his upper lip and eye swollen. A large bruise and cut dominated the left side of his face, where he had been on the receiving end of an angry boot. Making it back to the house, the couple ate as if they had not eaten in days. By the looks of them, they had probably not. The baby was just as hungry as he greedily sucked down the evaporated milk.

It seems that some people did not judge others by the content of their character but by the color of their skin. Those people wanted Juan and his family out of the neighborhood and had sent Juan a very clear message: leave.

The new conversation began that evening. Jason, Jeb, and Officer Henry discussed among themselves what to do with Juan and his family. As it was now, the three families seemed to have enough to make it past the winter. Even thrive. Juan's family seemed nice enough. He seemed like a hard worker. But what about others who wanted to stay? What was to be expected if someone chose to stay? What would be the rules? Who would decide those rules? The discussion opened so many questions, but some things were determined. Those allowed to stay at Bo Hill would be hardworking and moral people. Also, anyone staying here would not be receiving government assistance.

Why not allow people receiving SNAP benefits to stay? Because it would open the doors to government search without just cause. "Just cause." From the local reports he had heard on the radio, "just cause" and "due process" were antiquated concepts for the government. The residents of Bo Hill would not comply with tyranny, nor would they surrender their means of defense.

Why was the United States government abusing its powers? Marshal law had been declared. The government was on the verge of forcing all Americans to register for public assistance, which consequently would suspend most of their constitutional rights. In addition, federal government seemed less concerned with protecting citizenry and more concerned with maintaining and seizing power. But why? What had caused the federal government to act this way?

The present state of the federal government seemed to be the direct result of an erosion of citizen rights. With the "Great Society" of the 1960's, the federal government enacted numerous welfare programs, providing the poor with cash, food, and housing with the hope of lifting the poor from poverty. With such high hopes, five federal housing projects had been constructed in Jason's hometown of Tuckerville, being christened with beautiful names such as "Forest Grove" and "Eastside Gardens."

The results of the "Great Society" were evident to anyone. Children were taught to fail evaluations in order to qualify for supplemental assistance. Adults did the same to qualify for disability. Women were encouraged to have children out of wedlock. And no one sought employment. The housing projects had become breeding grounds for unemployment and crime. Needless to say, no one referred to the housing project in Tuckerville as "Eastside Gardens."

Then there were the "Wars." In 1990's, the "War against Drugs" allowed the government to seize properties of anyone with drug charges. People simply sat by as the property rights of citizens were eroded. Then, in the wake of 9/11, President Bush and Congress patriotically signed the Patriot Act, having declared the "War" against terror. Those who spoke out against the federal government were socially ostracized for not being blindly patriotic. In truth, the Patriot Act allowed the federal government to commit espionage against its own citizens. Although vehemently denying it, the IRS had worked hand-in-hand with the NSA, threatening and terrorizing people who spoke out against the establishment.

Before the Tuesday meltdown, there was even a law that had been enacted called "The Affordable Care Act." The law promised free healthcare, but only offered government-funded discounts to those who "financially qualified." Anyone who dared to oppose this healthcare law by pointing out the past welfare failures was dismissed as racist and mean-spirited.

No, the current state of affairs with the U. S. government, or whatever remained of that government, was a direct result of it seizing power and doing anything to keep that control. At least that was the conclusion reached by the three men at the dining room table that evening.

The next morning, after the family had rested, the trio talked with Juan. Juan told the men he and his family were here to harvest the cotton crop in the next county. Juan had originally claimed to be from south Texas, but when questioned by Jason, Jeb, and Henry, he admitted being from Matamoras, right across the border.

"I stay wintertime this year and help with planting. I drive tractor and combine. Do anything. My boss let me stay in that trailer. My boss is dead now, though. He was killed."

"Why didn't you go to town and get food?" Jason asked.

"Because people see me and say I take their job. I did take *no* jobs. He always hire me since I work hard. But they shoot when they see me."

"Have you ever been arrested?" Officer Henry probed, watching the Hispanic's eyes.

"No, sir," Juan answered truthfully. Henry nodded. His experience as a police officer gave him the uncanny ability to determine if a person was telling the truth. He was satisfied. They all were. It mattered little where Juan and his family were from, nor did matter the color of their skin. What did matter was that Juan was an honest, hardworking, moral individual.

Juan, his wife, and child moved in the next day. They resided in one of two remaining houses opposite the Henry residence. Juan's knowledge of farming might prove invaluable in the months to come.

* * *

William

Juan had brought a question to Jason's mind, one that had been nagging at him since the Tuesday Meltdown. What had become of his oldest son? William, his wife, and daughter were fine when the phones had gone down, but that had been almost a month ago. William's family was living on the edge of Middleton. Since then, however no news, nothing. The family had talked about a "rescue mission" of sorts for some time. This afternoon, however, was the time for action. There were enough people at Bo Hill to defend it against what problems had occurred recently. Jason would take his two sons that evening. They would travel the 12 miles to Middleton and find his oldest son. They would bring William and his family back if that was what William wanted.

Philip's black GMC Sonoma was small and the right color for night travel. Its lights had been duct taped up where there were no lights showing, minus two shaded slits, which served as blackout drive. The Sonoma, like many model trucks, had automatic lights but these could be turned off by simply applying the emergency brake one click down, changing the vehicle from military blackout drive to lights out. There had been some discussion on disabling the headlights altogether, but that idea quickly came to an end when the prospect of high-speed getaway came up.

The plan was simple; the route planned. Move as close to William's apartment complex by vehicle; if possible, all the way. Avoid direct contact before arriving at William's place. Afterward, move back via the same route, again avoiding contact. Rally points were planned, memorized, and shared. If Jason and his sons did not make it back within 48 hours, Tim would travel with Haley for support or assistance. No other families would be involved. It was Jason's family; therefore it was Jason's responsibility.

In the cab of the truck, Jason drove while Peter rode shotgun. Technically, Peter rode 9mm carbine. Jason was traveling with his 9mm Browning pistol holstered on his chest, and 5 spare mags in his BDU jacket. His SKS and ammo belt were behind the seat. Jason had been insistent on using military grade web gear to carry ammunition, and now 4 ammo pouches boasted 120 rounds of 7.62x 39mm full metal jacket with another 200 rounds in an ammo can. In the back, Philip was ready to rock. A 2"x4" frame had been constructed to mount a low back seat of an office chair securely. When strapped in, Philip had "gun-rests" nails on the lumber to steady the semiautomatic shotgun, which was loaded with slugs. Both it and another loaded shotgun were secured to Philip via dog leash and duct tape. Philip sported a belt of shotgun shells around his shoulder as well, with both slug and double-aught buckshot. Philip was ready to take out any and all pursuers.

Traveling at dark was a slow procedure. Jason stuck to the route, gravel roads, avoiding towns altogether. This involved a rather circuitous route around the southeast of town. Crossing the interstate would be necessary. Where to cross was another question. If possible, they would simply go over the overpass. If not, crossing the interstate directly might work. If all else failed, parking the vehicle as close as possible and traveling by foot would open up more options. Jason hoped it would not come down to traveling that far by foot. That would mean over three miles, one way.

Arriving near the interstate, Jason slung his SKS and moved through a drainage ditch toward the overpass. The ditch was dry which meant they could probably drive the small pickup cross-country if necessary. The overpass appeared deserted. One could never be too careful, however. Jason high crawled to the south side of the overpass. From there he could see a glare ahead at the first Middleton exit 4 miles away. Here, however, seemed dark enough to cross. He was invisible in the shadows as he rushed across the first two lanes, then the next. He did not want to chance driving the pickup along the top of the bridge. Anyone could see such a silhouette. However, in the median next to the overpass, a track joined the two lanes, being marked "Emergency Vehicles Only." Jason chuckled silently; certainly his vehicle qualified for this. After jumping the far fence, scanning for possible sentries, and finding a navigable trail for the black Sonoma, Jason doubled back, cutting through the wire fence and pulling it back as he returned.

The Sonoma was almost as black as the shadows hiding it as the trio drove across the four-lane highway. The plan was to continue driving rather quickly down the gravel roads, knowing there would be barking dogs and nervous, trigger-happy families to avoid. This went according to plan.

William's apartment lay on the far side of the highway, opposite an industrial complex. As they approached the complex, Jason got out and walked alone, ahead of the vehicle. The National Guard Reserve Center was located there, and it appeared occupied. Evidently, those stationed there were patrolling the warehouses. Jason, a veteran himself, was sympathetic with the National Guard, and wanted to avoid a run-in with local guardsmen and any potentially deadly misunderstandings.

"We'll park here behind these elms." The darkness covered the entire vehicle. The tinted windows would not usually reflect too much light, but still the entire vehicle was covered with heavy canvas.

"Peter. You stay here. Wait." Jason handed him another weapon, a Ruger 10/22, its stainless body camouflaged with dark clay and effectively silenced with a metal-cased oil filter. "No kills except in self-defense. Abandon the vehicle if it is discovered by military. We will find another way."

Peter was given one of the Scooby-Doo radios, turned most of the way down. The radio toys had been effective up to 5 miles over flat fields. Jason hoped they would operate well enough over the one mile remaining between the vehicle and William's house.

Jason and Philip made their way on foot, Jason in lead, Philip trailing. "Buddy ready... buddy moving," Jason thought of the old basic training phrase as he signaled Philip on toward a lit area near Highway 18. It seemed some of Middleton had electricity again. Suddenly, vehicle lights swept the limestone gravel and concrete parking lot right when Philip had moved up toward his father. Phillip barely managed to evade the patrol vehicle, its lights pointed toward the corner of the building where the father and son lay prone, rifle and shotgun pointed at the potential aggressors.

Talking was heard from the Humvee. Two black-clad men, not Guardsmen, were laughing. Mounted from the top, a .50 caliber machine gun was manned by a third. The two moved around the warehouse, avoiding contact. It had been a good idea to park the half-mile behind and continue on foot. Their poor Sonoma was no match for the Hummer. The .50 caliber rounds from the mounted gun could literally chew through the compact truck and its occupants. Where it was considered against the laws of war to use .50 caliber rounds on personnel, the federal government had apparently pulled off the silk gloves to deal with opposition.

Nearing the highway, Jason high-crawled up to the edge of the road to recon the far side, where the apartment complex lay. There was a roadblock about 400 meters west, toward town. If they attempted to cross the road, they would be seen. Jason had already reckoned as much. He had known there was a culvert underneath the highway, about 100 yards from a closed convenience store.

Making his way back to his waiting son, the two rushed around the dimly lit metal warehouse and made their way through the ditch. This ditch was not dry, and the water stank of death and sewage. Having to crouch in the water as they moved toward the culvert, Philip saw the body first. A woman, lay face up, naked and bloated from decay. He pulled back, exhaled sharply and gagged. As Jason crawled past, he had no choice but to push the body to the side with his SKS. Putrid gas exuded from the body, making Jason wanting to gag as well. "Still, move on," Jason thought.

The culvert was 26 inches high, which was definitely navigable, but meant getting wet. Jason removed his BDU jacket and wrapped his SKS for noise discipline. Philip did the same. There was no protecting the weapons from the water, however. Fortunately, both the SKS and Hi-point 9mm carbine were extremely reliable, even in less than desirable circumstances. The putrid water under Highway 18 definitely qualified as "less than desirable." Jason had placed the walkie-talkie in a plastic bag and hoped it would stay dry.

Out the other side, being careful not to be impatient and make noise, Jason moved close to the ditch bank and took up a prone fighting position, waiting for his son. The highway above was lit, unlike the ditch where Jason lay, but he could still discern Philip's face; his son was smiling. Philip had always heard William brag about crawling through a culvert with his dad. Philip finally had the chance to do the same. "Hopefully William, Tamera, and baby Savannah would be able to make the same journey back," Jason thought.

The apartment complex was dark, but there were some fires on street intersections. Best go around the complex and come in through the alley, behind William's duplex. Although it took more time, the route they took was without incident and they arrived in William's back yard. Jason pulled out a thick black Sharpie and white plastic tarp. On it he wrote, "Let us in. It's Dad and Philip!" He sprinted to the side of the house with the tarp and two pieces of duct tape.

Let's just hope I am not shot by my own son, Jason thought. He silently duct taped the two corners of the sign to the sliding glass door, knocked three times loudly on the glass, and then jumped back prone into the grass. And waited.

Nothing. One minute passed. Two. Then, the curtain moved slightly. An imperceptible light inside, then the curtain moved again. Pause. A flashlight beam. Then, an open door. "Dad?"

Life in Middleton had changed to a life of compromise. The compromise was this. The "Neighborhood Watch" took your food and agreed not to shoot you. These thugs had taken charge two weeks ago. William had the foresight to bury his shotgun in the backyard after he saw his neighbor, who was not so agreeable to the merits of compromise, shot along with his wife. The neighborhood watch was apparently in league with the black-clad military types, Homeland Security, who were patrolling the streets around the industrial complex. The Neighborhood Watch kept the neighborhood in line, and Homeland Security looked the other way when certain indiscretions such as theft, rape, and murder occurred. William had very little food left. Everything in the house had been taken. Only that which William had put in a pillowcase and thrown in the ditch survived.

"Dad, I tried to come to you, but we weren't allowed to leave. Word has it that Department of Homeland Security is going to relocate us. Some say they want workers for the factories. Nobody knows. The first thing those guys took were the radios. Even took out or shot the ones in the cars."

"Son, would you and Tamera consider moving to our place? I sure would love to have you at Bo Hill." William nodded.

"Dad, they do bad things to you if you are caught outside at night."

"Yeah, son, I noticed. Dress in layers, no polyester shell clothing. Makes too much noise. You are going to get dirty."

"What about Savannah?" Tamera was worried.

"You have no food here. Savannah must go. But if Savannah starts crying, it could cost us our lives. What can you do?"

"The watch does not know about Savannah, or they would have taken all her food as well. I gave Savannah Benadryl and hid her in the back when the watch searched our home last time."

"Well, if she handled that once, now might be a good time to try it again."

As the group readied themselves, Jason handed Tamera his 9mm Browning. "It sounds like DHS does not take prisoners. Point and shoot." Tamera nodded, baby Savannah strapped to her chest, and the 9mm in her hand.

"No talking, no noise. You are going to get messy. But we are going home. I love you."

As they left the apartment the back way, a woman was screaming nearby. No doubt, courtesy of the neighborhood watch. He could not rescue the entire neighborhood. They were outgunned. Still a shiver went through the entire group as the screaming continued. He had no choice. "Avoid contact. Accomplish the mission. Move on." --For now.--But this horror must not be allowed to continue...

Jason tried the cheap walking-talkie "Dad," Peter answered, "There is an Army truck close by. I am hiding. I don't think they have seen the truck yet." The family had already made their way through the foul-smelling culvert. Baby Savannah had peacefully snoozed the entire time, strapped under her mother who crawled hands and knees through 5 inches of sewer, a 9mm hanging around her neck. Now that they were out the other side of the culvert, and having regrouped, Jason's mind began to swim. What if Peter was discovered? What if they all were? Jason knew the answer, but that was not acceptable. Think.

"Peter, we will rally at your location."

Maybe they could get in the truck and stealth away. What did they have? Two semiautomatic shotguns, William's pump shotgun, an SKS, a 9mm carbine, and a silenced .22, plus another .22 if they could make it to the truck. More than enough firepower for an ambush if the hummer wasn't armored. Why chance it? That hummer could make mincemeat of the lot of them. Better go on foot.

There was gunfire and laughter ahead. "Oh, God, they've found Peter." Jason, William, and Philip began a sprint toward the voices, the others following. In the headlights of the Humvee stood a woman and a man, hands raised. Then a single gunshot. More laughter as the man fell. The evil bastards were no better than the animals that had invaded Jason's home.

DHS apparently had their vices, as they walked toward the kneeling, weeping woman. That would be one vice too many, if the Hamilton family had anything to say about it, though. Slowing to a walk, firearms raised, the father and sons moved slowly forward, weapons trained and blazing. One black-clad fellow was thrown backward by a shotgun blast, yet was getting up. Body armor. A three round burst from Philip, who carried the 9mm carbine put him down. A round from Jason's SKS knocked the second down, and apparently knocked the breath out of him.

The third man made his way to the side of the armored Humvee. He began firing a 9mm and was apparently attempting to operate the radio. Something like a loud cough sounded several times. The DHS agent fell. "It's me, dad. I got 'em." Peter walked out carrying the silenced .22. Jason took the silenced .22, placed its muzzle atop the head of the one living DHS agent, still struggling to get up. Jason looked at William, Philip, and Peter. "Guilty?" The three boys slowly nodded in turn. Jason fired twice into the DHS agent's temple.

The woman still knelt, weeping for her husband. She was in her thirties, and apparently life had not been good to either her or her murdered husband in the last month. Her face, grief-stricken, was hollow from hunger. She could not speak nor could she stop weeping.

"We take the bodies and the vehicle, everything. The woman can come with us. Philip, you take the truck behind me." William, take shotgun with me. Tamera, is Savannah okay?"

"I think so."

"Blackout drive. Follow me. Remember rally points, just in case."

Jason's mind was swimming. He had just engaged the federal government. The United States of America. What had he done? ...He had done right. It was the government who was at fault. He had little choice. Any law-abiding citizen...no...that was wrong...any decent person would have done exactly the same. All of this was incriminating. The vehicle, the weapons, the bodies. Could the radio be traced? Was the vehicle marked or tracked?

As they drove down the gravel road, the lights of the National Guard Center were lit up. What role did they play in this? Did they have blood on their hands as well. Jason knew several people in the 877th Engineer Battalion. It was hard to believe that SSG Moses or SSG Jones were guilty of war crimes.

The Hummer would remain hidden in a metal building until it could be searched from top to bottom. The weapons, however, would be immediately appropriated, including the .50 caliber. Jason would talk with someone about what he had seen. Maybe someone from the 877th · As Jason drove, suddenly he felt that his family was very exposed. Ariel surveillance, including drones, made it possible to view everything from the air. Were they being watched right now?

* * *

New Residents

A full day had passed since they had escaped with William, Tamera, and Savannah. One-year-old Savannah was hanging on the furniture and standing up in the living room. A fire was on and the teakettle was boiling water for coffee. Right now, it was easy enough to brew coffee by pouring boiling water over the coffee filter of the automatic drip coffee maker, which meant it wasn't exactly an automatic coffee maker anymore. Oatmeal was an easy fix for breakfast. William didn't normally appreciate oatmeal, nor did his father when he was younger but both appreciated it now. William, appreciated it simply for the food and heat; his father, for a breakfast with his oldest son.

After breakfast, father and son went to stand a four-hour watch on Bo Hill. The day was bright and cold. The mercury had read 27 degrees that morning, and smoky breath rose from the two as they talked. "DHS had some serious gear in that hummer," Jason started. "They had 3 fully automatic M4 assault rifles, pistols, and full combat load of ammo. Guess what they had in the back."

"Huh?"

"Two AT-4s and a case of grenades. Straight military issue."

"Oh, yeah?" William said, not really into the conversation.

"Son, is everything okay? Why don't you tell me what happened in Middleton?"

"We did not see too many of those DHS guys. Either there weren't very many of them, or they hardly ever came by the apartments. We tried to just stay home."

Jason simply nodded and listened.

"It all started when I was trying to go for food one day. They said

Kroger was open. So when we tried to leave the apartment complex, this group of thugs with yellow bandanas on their sleeves had the front entrance blocked. When I pulled up, a big guy pulled a shotgun on us and said to go back and stay inside. That he would be by later and explain things. It was a week before he did come by. Things happened. I couldn't stop it." There were tears in William's eyes. When he could, he continued. "Savannah was outside. We had hid her there. When they finally left, I got her.... I couldn't stop it, Dad!" William twisted his hands into fists, his face struggling to contain the emotion, but he was otherwise still.

"William, had you pulled your gun, you would have all been killed."

"Did I do right, Dad? William managed.

"You did good, son. You're here now." Jason's arm went over his son's shoulder. "That's over now." Both had seen horrible days since that one Tuesday, and more were soon to come, but this was not one of those days. As the cold sun beat down on father and son, the years that they had spent apart melted away. Somehow, this pain and tragedy of the last month had healed their wounded relationship.

Things had already changed at Bo Hill. Robert and Sue Everling, along with their grown son and daughter, had returned. There had been problems in the Ozark foothills as well. If they were to weather a storm, at least they would do so at home. Jason talked with Robert.

"I do have a bank payment to make next September for the crops. I don't know how I am going to make it considering there ain't enough seed for cotton, nor enough fuel, insecticide, fertilizer. Heck, Jason, the bank I make my payment to is gone, burned down. I don't know what to do or how to do it."

"Well, I appreciate what you did for my family and me. Most of the families along the ridge ran off when those ex-cons came through, but maybe now people will come back. We are trying to figure what to plant. Juan here says we should plant corn."

"Corn plants easy; it doesn't yield as much profit unless you get subsidies. If I had fuel, I would say rice. But that takes a lot of water and levees need to be cut. You can plant, tend, and harvest corn by hand easier. I do have a good strain of corn seed. 60 bushels. Paid near $240 a bushel for it. That should plant about 180 acres."

"Well I don't have a lot of money, Robert. But lately money doesn't seem to be doing anyone much good."

Robert let out a simple laugh. "Well, you don't need that much, Jason. That much could yield 32,000 bushels."

"It ain't just for us, Robert. People are hungry. We could trade with it."

"It's Roundup Corn, but I don't know if I can get much Roundup the way things are. It ain't sweet corn, but it should cook and grind both."

"Do you have anything that could mill the corn once we harvest?" Robert grinned again.

It was agreed. Robert would provide seed for a corn crop, equipment, and know-how. In return, a vehicle would post on Pine View Road, providing security. Robert became the official agricultural consultant for the community of Bo Hill. Juan's job would be to coordinate with Robert to get a crop into the ground. Robert also agreed to help find seed for some garden crops.

Four groups of people came seeking refuge at Bo Hill over the next week. One group of four people was turned away at the barricade. Drug users. After careful evaluation, the three other groups were accepted. A promise was made by each and every one in the groups to improve and defend Bo Hill to their very last breath.

The cold was moving in, and blankets were issued. 4 55-gallon metal barrels were fabricated into wood-burning stoves and installed in the living rooms. Axes were issued. There was wood to collect, from the nearby woods. Rice from the Everling farm was gratefully received. Six men, four women and three teenagers were added to the watch, which greatly relieved the stress of sentry duty. They were issued shotguns and rounds both for hunting and for defense. This brought the levy at Bo Hill to a total of 26. Yet this also meant 26 mouths to feed.

Jason was the only family with any livestock, none of which had been touched save the one sheep last month. If the herd were to grow, the livestock must be kept that way. Untouched. Peter had become quite proficient with snares, using thin tie wire to make small loops at narrow parts of rabbit trails. Possums and raccoons apparently had a taste for the persimmons behind the house, and Philip successfully set live traps in the woods and ditch banks. As a result, many early days that winter saw the family eating meat. Deborah found possum distasteful at first, saying they looked like rats. It seemed, however, that the days of purchasing "fresh" meat at the store and placing it in the refrigerator were gone. Storing fresh meat now meant keeping a raccoon or possum live in a cage and letting the meat clean itself out before the animal became lunch.

Meetings were held every Tuesday and Friday at 7:00 p.m. At the meetings, Peter would show others how he managed to snare and clean small game. Margarita would show how she would prepare various recipes and cook over the open fire. One man was a welder by trade, and worked with Tim fabricating metal in a welding shop by the northern barricade. Juan's wife Maria became the best of friends with Margarita, and the two would often be conversing in Spanish, as that was the only language Maria spoke.

One issue Juan brought up was the spring crop. In about 120 days, a corn crop would be planted. Juan spoke of how the fields could be used.

Tactics of patrol movement, weapons training, house clearing, and basic first aid were taught at night when possible, and in the woods during the day. OPEC became important. Defensive fallback positions were set up, and drills were conducted. Bo Hill would not be caught off guard. The barricades at both ends of Bo Hill were changed, with the vehicles being moved. The fallen trees remained but in place of the vehicles were a series of cables pulled across the road every evening. Although the cable system could effectively knock any vehicle out of control, it was virtually invisible from the air.

Better than any defense, however, Jason knew Bo Hill needed a good offense. Like it or not, Jason had effectively declared war against the federal government. Jason worried about the repercussions.

The hummer had been searched from top to bottom at Robert's farm and no tracking device had been found. Still Officer Henry insisted the radio be unmounted and placed under a pile of tin. Somehow the group had managed to stash 6 of the 8 vehicles under carports, the two outbuildings, and the shed. Two more were at the Henry residence next door. Soon, Juan was to have his own truck, but that was not yet. The dump truck had been moved forward in the shed to make room for the newest edition, an armored Humvee complete with a .50 caliber machine gun and a heavy 600-round load. With proper positioning, the M2 could effectively guard both barricades around Bo Hill against any vehicle save heavy armor.

* * *

Oak Ridge and DHS

The day was Thursday, not that it really mattered. What did matter was that today five people from Bo Hill were traveling to Oak Ridge. To avoid any questions, they were traveling in their newly-acquired military vehicle. All but Officer Henry were wearing military uniforms. And all five, Jason, Officer Henry, William, Philip, and Tim, had received haircuts, nice military ones. Margarita had done the honors with Jason's clippers, which were plugged into a power inverter. Tim had made quite a protest before he sat down, but he finally had his "ears lowered" as well. The three youth wore body armor. Officer Henry, who had never fired a .50 caliber but was a quick study, manned the weapon while the three boys rode armed for patrol. Each of them had an M4 while Jason sported the M16A2. All had 9mm pistols and grenades. There was even an AT4 in the back. They were ready to take on an army. No one yet realized they would actually be taking on an army that very day.

Their destination was the National Guard Armory in Oak Ridge. Although the 877th had its headquarters in Middleton, there were company-sized centers both in Bartersville and nearby Oak Ridge. Since Oak Ridge was only 6 miles away, they would travel to that National Guard center.

Questions needed to be answered such as what role did the 877th have in supporting DHS? Were friends and colleagues that Jason had in the National Guard now turned enemies? Ten minutes of driving brought the Humvee to the junction at the end of Highway 167. There a state patrolman standing in front of his cruiser facing the hummer. He walked up beside the driver's side, fully aware that his meager arsenal was no match for the crew.

"Can I help you, soldier?"

"MSG Hamilton here to see Alpha Company, 877th."

"Ain't hardly anybody left there. Besides, why should I let you in here?"

"Officer, I have a duty to perform, and neither hell nor high water will keep me from it. No offense, but neither will you. We are good men simply looking for answers."

The officer studied them for a minute. "You know where it's at?"

Jason nodded to his right at the building.

The patrolman nodded back. "I will be here when you get back. See me if you need anything else."

As they rolled up the hill to Alpha Company headquarters, a man in civilian clothes came out of the building to meet them. Anxiously, the man came out to the vehicle, not too close, and almost shouted "They said that those who were able to deploy should go to Middleton. We don't have anyone here," a certain SSG Mosby stated. Then there was recognition in his eyes, and a slow smile ran across his face. "Well Mr. Hamilton, umm I mean Master Sergeant Hamilton," addressing Jason by his rank.

"Good to see you, Mr. Mosby." Mr. Mosby had volunteered to help with football in Tuckerville, Jason's hometown. Jason had seen him on the sidelines earlier this year, cheering on the home team, which had needed all the help they could get.

"Hey, Mosby, can we talk? Is anyone listening?"

"Umm, I know what you mean." Mosby was always shifting from leg to leg nervously, but this time he seemed to have a reason to do so as he looked around.

Mosby signaled Jason to drive behind him to park. Jason did so, backing in while Officer Henry remained vigilant at the machine gun. Backing in to park, Jason got out with Officer Henry, who let Philip man the gun, while William took the driver's seat. Peter was outside with his M4, guarding their six.

Mosby lit up a cigarette under the smoking cabana. Although Jason was tempted to light one up as well when offered, he declined. No need to start up another bad habit, especially one he might not be able to maintain. Mosby began, "When they called us up, I thought it was just to maintain order. I mean, we do that, don't get me wrong. We got us some of those bastards that had escaped from jail doing all that killing down Highway 167. I guess the rest escaped."

Both Jason's and Officer Henry's expressions were poker-faced. Escaped?...Not exactly.

"But after that, DHS called us to Middleton. Apparently they wanted us to do their bitch work, keeping us busy. If you ask me, they want the battalion under their thumb so the 877th will stay out of their way. They deploy them without weapons except to guard Wal-Mart and Kroger. The people here in Oak Ridge need all the help they can get, and there is only the sheriff and two deputies here. To be honest with you, I don't trust them, either. The other police officers have gone home to protect their families. Can't blame 'em. The entire west side of town has been quarantined. The volunteers, well, they burn the bodies during the day. At night, families sleep together and hope for the best."

"So the entire unit is gone to Middleton?"

"Yeah, about 20 or so are over there; the rest said to hell with this shit and went home."

Now it was Jason's turn. He recounted to Mosby the shooting he had witnessed in Middleton, and what William had witnessed. Mosby listened, slack-jawed. He went to take a drag only to realize he had dropped his cigarette a moment before.

"Those bastards."

"Yeah," Jason replied quietly. "Why are you still here, Mosby?"

"Well, my wife is here, too, actually. You know Toshia is away in California with her husband. I haven't heard from her lately. This place seemed a lot safer than staying in Tuckerville, so when they called me up, which was right before those ex-cons went on their killing spree, I reckoned the Mrs. could take the drive with me. We have cots here, but since SSG Moses left yesterday with the last six men, I was wondering what we were going to do. Been keeping guard the best we can, but with only us both... Let's just say when I saw that maw deuce on your vehicle, I got a bit nervous."

They moved into the building.

"So, the men left, but they didn't want them armed?" Jason reflected.

"Yeah, right. It seemed sort of funny to me, too."

"It seems to me they wanted the National Guard defenseless."

"I doubt any of the boys would ever do shit like what you saw," Mosby said defensively.

"Most wouldn't. Some might, though. Maybe sending for your men in small groups like that was intentional. Some kind of culling process."

"Culling," Mosby remarked. "That's like weeding out the bad ones, right?"

"Or the good ones. Have you heard from anyone in your unit?"

"Not recently. I had good radio contact with SSG Moses till this morning. He said he was pulling in the gate and that he would radio me back. Never did. Come to think of it, Captain MacDonald said he would call back with a frequency change last week when he left. He never did, either. But I never could stand his ass, so I was happy just not to hear from him. Been getting communication with some "Head Agent" in Middleton telling us to send them men.

"Mosby, I saw the reserve center. People are there; vehicles are running. I just didn't see any Guardsmen. Now Mosby, why did you stay back again?"

"The arms room. Security is down so they needed someone here."

"If they wanted it secure, they would have left more than one man here, Mosby. Seems, they wanted you alone."

"Hell, that's what I told them. Why would that DHS agent want me here alone? ...Son of a bitch. Do you think they want the weapons and ammo for themselves?"

"If you want, you can come stay with us. Something tells me if DHS does show up, it won't be pleasant."

"I am not leaving my post. Period. What the hell have those sumsofbitches done with my unit. Oh, if they show up, I have enough here to keep them busy for a while."

"This ain't the movies, Mosby. If they are wanting the arms room, you will be gunned down. Think about it. What about your wife?..."

"Can she stay with you?"

"I ain't gonna be a widow-maker."

"Hell, I owe it to my unit to stand my post. I am staying."

Jason thought a moment. DHS knew SSG Mosby would be alone today. It looked as though they had planned it that way. If DHS wanted the weapons and explosives, they would show up today. "Mosby, if you make your stand here, we will stand with you," Jason said simply. "Besides, they are probably only expecting one person," Jason continued, placing his hand on the shorter man's shoulder. "I hope we are both wrong about this, though."

The moment of decision passed, and the three realized how few moments they might have left. They made their way down to the arms room.

"What do you have here anyway?" Jason asked.

"Just M16s, SAWs, and ammo. We got a couple of older M60s we never turned in. Hell, and worlds of 7.62 mm belt ammo for those old puppies. Oh, there is the shape charges and C-4."

"Really?"

"Well what did you expect? We are a combat engineer company."

Officer Henry ran out to get the boys and move the hummer. He parked behind the dumpster. Only the maw deuce was visible above. This he trained on the road entrance. The boys ran to the drill hall, where Jason and Mosby stood waiting for them with two M60s and two cans of ammo. Mosby and Jason had their own load as well: two shaped charges, det cord, two M60 igniters, and a pair of crimpers. They had little time to lose.

About thirty minutes later, three military hummers were stopped by the police sentry on the road below. It was the burst of small arms fire which had caused everyone to notice. Mosby and Jason both saw the highway patrolman fall. As the hummers pulled into the Alpha Company entrance, none seemed to notice the M985 HEMTT pulling behind them, effectively blocking the drive. SSG Mosby was prone behind four sandbags with an M60 trained at the lead vehicle. He raised, taking a knee, asking what the lead driver wanted. Dark-uniformed men began to get out and train their assault rifles on his position. Mosby dropped flat as he took automatic small arms fire. "Oh, shit," he muttered, hitting the ground.

Coming to Mosby's aid, Officer Henry opened up with the maw deuce from the hilltop, literally chewing through the first armored hummer and into the men still inside. The other two hummers quickly emptied, with twelve agents finding makeshift fighting positions. Their defense, however, was pitifully inadequate. Jason and Mosby opened up with two M60s, mowing down four of the DHS agents while eight managed to return fire from behind the hummers. Jason called out "Fire in the hole." Both he and Mosby pulled the igniters simultaneously, taking cover behind their sandbags. A tremendous boom immediately shook the ground. The entire world seemed to stop in a ringing silence that followed. There was no need for more gunfire. The shape charges had been a game stopper.

The hummers had actually been moved sideways by the force of the shaped charges. It had been Mosby's idea to place 6 boxes of empty brass in front of the charges after digging the two cone-shaped explosives in the ground. The result were two field-expedient claymore mines with about 6 times the blast. One such device would have been overkill. Their result was 18 DHS agent casualties. Actually, perhaps it was more accurate to say DHS casualty remains. The bodies near the blasts were simply a mass of cloth and meat, held together by fragment-laden body armor. No one could have survived. Even from 200 feet away, one of Jason's ears was bleeding from the blast. Those on the north side had encountered the M60 machine guns as well. Body armor was no match for 7.62 mm ammunition. It was war, and war was horrible. Officer Henry had come down from the top of the hill, weapon drawn unnecessarily. "Man, we really fucked them up."

"They fucked with my family first," Jason replied quietly.

The first DHS vehicle was not salvageable. Armored or not, .50 caliber rounds from the M2 had effectively dead-lined the vehicle along with the 4 passengers inside. The other two hummers, however, were still salvageable, although the blasts had exploded two of their tires. A scavenge for weapons, ceramic plate body armor, helmets and other useful items began. M4s, the Army's more compact version of the M16, were recovered along with several OD green plastic cases. Peter found something Jason had only seen videos of. "What's that dad," Peter asked.

"That, son, is the AA-12, a fully automatic shotgun." Evidently, these DHS agents had come to clean house, no matter who was to get in their way. Had Jason, Henry, and the boys come upon them at close quarters, things would have been ugly. Inside the cases, AT-4s. Two rocket launchers per vehicle was standard DHS issue. Odd.

In the midst of the carnage, no one noticed that SSG Mosby had gone back inside the drill hall. A few moments later, they heard "Hey guys, come here." Jason could see SSG Mosby at the top of the hill. As they gathered, they noticed the stunningly beautiful young brunette, at least ten years his younger, with the Staff Sergeant. Mosby had a silly, puppy dog smile on his face. "Guys, I would like you to meet my wife, Brenda." Apparently SSG Mosby was one hundred percent, certifiably...in love.

That evening it was discussed what should happen. Mosby and Jason would take a DHS vehicle, both of which were fully operational after two tires were changed out. All scavenged items were to belong to Bo Hill. SSG Mosby would continue to maintain responsibility for the National Guard facility, using its armament to defend the town of Oak Ridge. The armament consisted of 6 racks of M16s, fifteen cases of 5.56 mm, 8,000 rounds of 7.62 mm, 6 grenade launchers, 96 rounds of assorted HE, shotgun, and star cluster 4OMM grenades, 4 SAWs, and 2 M60 machine guns. In other words, enough firepower to arm a National Guard combat engineer company. In addition, the unit boasted 150 M112 bricks of C4, 16 shaped charges, 15 500-meter reels of detonation cord, and about 16 claymore mines, which apparently even Mosby had no idea were in there. Mosby's plan was to work in conjunction with the Sheriff and the one remaining deputy. In reality, the next day he, Officer Henry, and William, who stayed overnight with Mosby at the center, would end up shooting the sheriff, who would try to take the weapons by force. The deputy would never be heard from again.

More important was communicating with the combat engineer unit at Bartersville. The idea here was to make friends while they still could be made. An envoy should be sent out, a task for which Officer Henry immediately volunteered. "I already know the area. I used to drive by there every day."

Jason left that day with another hummer, a cache of weapons, and about 40 blocks of C4 with a reel of det cord, an M60 with 2000 rounds, and a M258 SAW with a basic combat ammunition load: Mosby's way of

Tuesday Meltdown

saying thank you. Jason would show Neb and Juan how to use the explosives and M60, and use some of the C4 to augment the north defensive line. More important, Jason left that day with an ally, someone he would not abandon. He planned to return to Oak Ridge tomorrow.

That evening, Jason instructed Jeb on plastic explosives and where to pre-position it at the barricades. Then Jason made his way back to the house. Deborah had hot chicken soup waiting for him, and brought it to the bedroom while he took off his boots.

"Honey, what happened today? Peter didn't say much except that William stayed there."

"We ran into a little trouble, but we handled it." Jason took a draw of the hot soup. Deborah's hands worked the knot in the back of his neck.

"I am worried about Peter. He doesn't talk much."

"He never talks much, baby.... The trouble in Oak Ridge. It was Homeland Security again. They tried to kill the soldier watching the armory. I think they wanted the weapons and no witnesses. Peter and I did talk on the way home. He just needs some time. He has seen a lot."

"Just lay back, Honey. Let me rub your back some, and..."

She was answered by snores. Jason was out for the night.

* * *

The Recon of Middleton

The next morning, Jason pulled back into town alone in the Dodge Ram. He was greeted by two men and one woman in military uniform. The woman walked up to the truck to greet him. As soon as she saw his name tag, she saluted, which was unusual since his rank was that of a non-commissioned officer. She informed him that SSG Mosby was at the unit and seemed proud that Jason had visited their post. As Jason drove past, he noticed in the mirror that the woman was whispering to the two men. They all stared at his departing vehicle.

SSG Mosby was in the motor pool with about 12 other men, "They wanted to join. I told them I could not pay them, but they say that didn't matter."

"Maybe its time you considered reforming Alpha Company of the 877th?"

The two spent about an hour talking about the threat. DHS would strike back, and they would come in force. They needed allies in this fight. People needed to know the truth. "We need video cameras. Small ones. They probably will have rechargeable ones at the high school. I will go into Middleton, along with two others. If any of us get caught, we will likely be immediately shot. Do you have any volunteers? Oh, and do you have a photocopy machine that runs around here? Pamplets might help get word out about what is going on.

Mosby volunteered for the espionage mission, but Jason noted everything that needed to be completed in Oak Ridge. It was Jason along with two other volunteers that left that evening after saying goodbye. Jason hugged William and said, "Tell Deborah I love her, and I'll be back soon." Then he left.

In the failing daylight, the men drove down what was known as "Old Military Road," a road which ran along the top of the narrow Andrew's Ridge. Cut in the Civil War by Union troops moving south, the road allowed the North to plug the Confederate batteries overlooking the Mississippi at Helena. Now creeping forward in a gray SUV, three "rebels" worked their way north. Rifles would stay in the car. A pistol and night vision goggles would accompany each man. In addition, each man carried a pen and paper plus one flip-style video camera. The plan was to record DHS atrocities committed against Middleton residents. A secondary mission was to find the location of the 877th. Finally, they were to gather any intelligence on DHS assets including possible retaliatory strikes against Oak Ridge. The three men parked the car at 11:00 p.m. on the outskirts of Middleton and were to meet back in 72 hours.

Jason left on foot, heading east, being armed with his Browning 9mm, a combat knife, and a desire to find the 877th. He skirted the bypass that bordered the city's south until he found a drain through which he could walk almost upright. Opening his backpack, he pulled out his night vision goggles, the AN PVS 4 system, not because he necessarily needed them, but because he wanted to conduct a second check of his equipment. The tunnel, pitch black, was lit with an eerie green glow as he moved his boots through the icy water and mud. Halfway through the conduit, he turned the goggles off and replaced them in the bag. He needed to develop night vision. Here he noticed that there was a side culvert, about 4 feet wide, and dry. It went back about 20 feet before veering upwards. Jason studied this room for a moment, realizing this place might make a convenient hideout if it could stay dry. Then he continued the remaining distance, coming out the other side, where the lighter shade of night seemed bright by comparison.

It was cold, but he was certain it would grow colder. Tonight, his first night of reconnaissance, showed a clear sky earlier with bright, cold stars. He walked past a baseball field complex in the darkness. The local school should be straight ahead. Avoiding contact and walking in the bitter cold reminded Jason of violating curfew up in Nova Scotia as a youth. Again, thirty years later, Jason was out past his assigned bedtime and challenging authority. Although the snow had melted, the cold was turning bitter in this neighborhood. That's when it struck him. No wood smoke. Certainly someone should be using wood for heat. If…the houses were occupied. The houses on this street seemed to be empty. And the only smell he could detect was…diesel. Up ahead of him, he could see a dirty stream of smoke rise, floating on its own heat, coming from the school.

The schoolhouse was occupied, and Jason wanted to answer that ever-nagging question "why." Fortunately, most older school houses had too many entrances and exits to make them a model of security. A window in an old part of the school maybe, Jason thought. Perhaps he could break one. Jason tried the side door, and it opened quietly. Well, that would work, too.

Inside was pitch dark. Jason reached for his night vision a second time that night. The hall was dark and cold, no emergency lights, no heat. Try a door. Locked. Quietly down to another door. Same. Then from up the hall, a dim light. Jason took off the goggles. Nothing. On again. Nothing. He had lost it. It was if someone had opened a door for a moment. His hand reached down to his holster and drew his Browning. He did not want to engage. If he did, his reconnaissance for these three days would be ruined. But he had to also avoid capture.

An Unexpected Rescue

There it was again, someone was coming back from across the hall into another room. Jason's clothing reflected little light and made little noise as he crept up the hall. Those army PT uniform pants were actually quite handy for such situations and, although it might not accessorize well with two hoodies and a pair of combat boots, the outfit was excellent for what Jason needed, moving stealthily. Some noise up ahead. A military-clad individual was carrying a clipboard and a flashlight. Jason shrank back. The uniformed man moved into the same room the other person had gone. It looked like the entrance to a gymnasium. Then two men left the entrance with a woman, who was crying. He followed behind them to what appeared to be a locker room.

"Hey, stop it. We just want to be friends. Look what we have here." One of the two men, a tall thin fellow with a drawn up face that appeared to look too small for his body, held up a snack bag of Doritos. The smile on the man's face was disgusting. The brown-haired woman was quite attractive, in spite of the fact that her face was gaunt from hunger. "Please, leave me alone. My husband works hard for you."

"Look slit, your two kids will starve if you do not cooperate. Maybe worse. Wait, how old is that cute little daughter of yours, eleven?" The other man watched with approval as the first man grabbed hold of the woman's hair and made her kneel. Neither man noticed Jason when he had entered the locker room a minute before. Only one of the men noticed when Jason simultaneously pulled back the one man's head and pushed the sharp tip of his combat knife up into the base of the man's skull. By then it was too late; the man went limp and Jason guided his body to the floor. The ungainly tall fellow was content finding his pleasure with the woman, oblivious to everything else. Jason would have quietly dispatched the second man, had the woman's eyes not turned and stared at him. The man turned around, exposing himself to Jason. Jason pointed at his indiscretion, and when the fellow looked down, Jason moved toward him quickly, whirling the knife. The tall man caught Jason's attack with his left hand, and grabbed Jason's face fiercely with his right, attempting to push his thumb into Jason's eye while tearing at Jason's cheek. Still Jason had momentum on his side, and his strong right arm found a place for the knife in the ungainly man's liver. The tall thin man seized up in pain, unable to even cry out. The dying man's grip on Jason relaxed as he stumbled back, his left hand groping to his side, where it drew back a stain of black blood. Eyes wide, the man attempted to say something but was unable.

All the while, the woman, still partially unclothed, watched in confusion. Jason reached to the ground and picked up her dirty Denver Bronco's sweatshirt, handed it to her, and put one finger over his mouth. The woman, with teary wide eyes, nodded.

"I am a friend. Can you tell me what is going on here?"
For the next five minutes the woman talked quietly. Jason had given her an MRE pound cake, which she ate while she talked. Her name was Destanee Chambers. She explained that her husband, along with some men had "been recruited" to service in the Department of Homeland Security. In short, the men had no choice but to work because DHS held their families at the school. She had seen her husband once since they took him. Food was scarce on the outside, but in the school, it was rationed even more. "To make them more manageable," Jason thought.

Jason realized what he had done. He had placed the lives of this woman and her children in danger. He had a single pistol with him. After all, this was not supposed to be a rescue operation. She could not go back and pretend this had not happened. People had seen her leave.

"How many men do they have here?"
"Three more are awake. There are 5 more sleeping. They change guard at eight in the morning."
"Weapons?"
"They have pistols and rifles."
"Look. I am one person here. I am not a rescue operation."
"If the guards see this, they will kill one of my children. Please."
Everyone needed help. Jason, however, simply could not help them all. But...he thought...Could he help these people? These people were not some inconvenience of Jason's plans; they were the reason for why Jason was here. So perhaps these people were not the 877th. But he could still help them...maybe.

If he could free these people, they would not be able to stay in Middleton. Their husbands lived and worked elsewhere. Hell, they needed rescue, too. In fact, the entire city of Middleton needed to be free.

"I will need your help."

The ugly tall guard had a pistol on him, a 9mm Glock. He would not be needing it anymore, so Jason chambered the weapon, holding it in his left hand. He then pulled a nightstick off the other dead body.

"The guard inside. Can you take care of him without causing noise? Kill him?"

"Well, I am pretty sure I can distract him. Tina might be able to help me. Gimme this." She pointed to his knife.

Jason waited by the door, pointing one gun at the principal's office, where two guards were, and the other at the classroom which housed the five sleeping guards.

Destanee had slipped inside again. She quietly woke her friend, who had been asleep with her 9-year-old son, and explained what was occurring. They both went up to the DHS agent guarding the gym. At first the guard was wary, hesitant. Tina whispered something in the guard's ear which made him smile and nod. Tina remained at the agent's neck while Destanee started to undo the guard's belt. He was quite distracted until Tina poked the tip of the combat knife under the guard's chin, drawing blood. With his trousers half open and hands up, Destanee unsnapped the pistol from the guard's belt, chambered a round, and shoved it to the man's groin. The guard, having lost all interest, remained quiet as the two women taped his hands, mouth, and feet, then shuffled him to the to the end of the hall.

The big question was how to eliminate the two remaining guards without alerting the five sleeping. In a perfect world, all plans are perfect. Here there was no clear answer. The two could walk out at any time, and Jason would have to fire, alerting the remaining guards. Hmm, fire....

Jason took the janitor's mop bucket and filled it with three old mop heads generously sprayed with Lysol, of which the janitor's closet still seemed to have an abundant amount. In went the shoes of the three guards, one still alive and duct-taped for silence and security. 5 full cans of Lysol Disinfectant Spray were added to the mix. Then came paper towel and fire. The black smoke partially filled the hallway before the classroom door could be opened and the makeshift firebrand wheeled inside under a bed. Then came the crash as a trophy case was pushed down in front of the classroom door. As if on cue, the two guards bolted out the door, assault rifles ready. They were immediately gunned down by Jason, Destanne, and Tina. The one bound guard watched wide-eyed as his buddies dropped and fell.

Inside the classroom, there were shouts from the five guards who had been roused from their sleep. The classroom filled up with smoke as the trapped men tried in vain to break open the door. One of the Lysol cans cooked off with a loud pop; then another. The water reserve for the sprinkler system, however, had long been drained by people in search of potable water. Shots were fired inside, and Jason dove, snatching an assault rifle just in time to see Tina's chest erupt in red. The smoke was thicker now.

"Stay here. Take cover and kill anything that comes out. Jason threw Destanne the other assault rifle. Then he ran out the front door. The outside windows, though not designed to be opened, were shattered by guards firing assault rifles as they attempted to escape the inferno. With two windows shattered, a person jumped through one of them, his shirt on fire. Half dressed, his bare feet and legs caught the window seal as he leapt out, causing his head to hit the outside brick wall. The smoke was thick now and, although the guards tried to provide covering fire for their escape, they were unable, being effectively blinded and choked by the black smoke. The bedding inside had caught fire by then and the classroom was ablaze. One at a time, the men jumped blindly out of the windows, weapons in hand, only to be shot by Jason. The last man threw his weapon out the window and had his hands raised to surrender. Jason consented.

Moving the prisoner in the hall, Jason asked about Tina. Destanne shook her head. What about her son inside? Who would take care of him. Enough. He had to move. The place was on fire, and although the classroom was containing it for now, it looked like the school was going up in smoke.

Destanne began the task of evacuating a gymnasium filled with confused people. Equipped with a flashlight, Destanne instructed them. "Get your clothes and shoes. Take your blankets." Destanne directed them outside.

"Where are your weapons?" Jason pointed to the second surviving guard, whose hands he had just secured with duct tape.

"In the office." The guard nodded toward where the other two guards had been.

" If you move from this spot, I will kill you. Do you understand?" Jason spoke simply, directly. Both men nodded. Jason then taped the second guard's legs together and moved inside the office. Inside were three rifles and three pistols. He slung the 5.56 mm rifles on his back and threw the pistols in his bag. Seeing the two ammo cans on the ground, he grabbed them, then he noticed the LBEs as well. Too many things, not enough time. He would come back if there was time.

When Jason slammed open the office door, one of the guards was almost out the door, trying to hop away. Jason shook his head. He dropped the ammo canister, leveled his Browning 9mm, and shot the man dead. Then he looked at the remaining guard. "Now, do *you* understand." The guard vigorously nodded an affirmative. Jason took the ammunition and weapons out to a tree by the sidewalk. Then he went back inside.

"Look, if you are useful, I will let you live." Jason had no intention of killing him, but the guard did not know that. "I am going to release your feet, follow me." Again, a nod. Jason used a piece of glass to cut through the duct tape holding the guard's feet and they both moved inside the office. Using the prisoner as a rack, Jason draped LBEs around his neck. Then he grabbed a duffel bag and began placing paperwork inside. There were some portable radios and what looked like an encrypted FM radio on the principal's desk. He then draped that duffel bag over the prisoner.

"Now, where is your transportation." Jason removed the duct tape from the prisoner's mouth. "On the other side of the gym. A hummer."

"Okay, let's take a look."

"Umm, we need the key. It's back inside," the guard volunteered.

Maybe this guy would be useful after all. "You are going to tell me everything you know. Where these womens' husbands work. Everything you can think of. We will find out how useful you really are."

A Long Walk

Destanee stood with Jason in the predawn darkness as the smoke billowed from the schoolhouse windows. It would soon be apparent that the school had been destroyed. At her side were her two children, shivering in the cold morning air. "Are you going to leave us here?" she asked. The children looked up at Jason, waiting for an answer.

"You can come with me," Jason replied. It was a simple plan. Take the hummer. Take the prisoner and the family. They could ride in the back.

"But what about them," the woman moved her hand to the crowd. "If you leave these people, they will be blamed."

Jason was taken back. Was she in her right mind? How could someone expect to escape and hide eighty people? The people were far too many to transport. They would have to walk. Where would they hide? Houses would surely be searched. And to make matters worse, it would be daylight soon. Even if by some miracle he could make it back to Bo Hill with these people, where would they stay? How could he ever expect to feed that number of people over the winter? Yet if he left the families at the school, they would certainly be caught. Punished. He should have left everything alone, provided for his own family....But he hadn't. He had already made the decision. Jason had to try.

Then Jason remembered the culvert where he had crossed under the highway. There had been a side culvert, enough room to stand. It was dry. Could the entire group hole up there for the day, and then move out tomorrow night. "Tonight," Jason corrected himself aloud. It was a risky plan, but moving 80 people in broad daylight was suicide. The culvert seemed to be their best chance. Jason hoped it would not rain.

"I need to address everyone."

Everyone listened as Jason spoke.

"It will be a long trip. It is risky. We will have to walk to avoid the patrols on the highway. I don't want to leave your husbands behind, but I wasn't prepared for a rescue mission, and we don't have much time. The sun will be up in an hour, but we have less time than that with this fire. We are traveling about two miles and then will take shelter. It will be cold and dangerous, and you must be quiet, no matter what happens. But if you choose to, you may come with me."

The group was quiet. Nobody wanted to face what might happen if they stayed. Jason simply started walking, with his prisoner beside him, and the group followed along behind.

No talking or noise is an extraordinary demand for 80 women and children that have just woken up to a gunfight and fire. Nevertheless the people understood the importance and moved rather quietly. In about 45 minutes, the group arrived, ragged, tired, and cold at the culvert. Dawn was almost breaking in the east. Jason picked a place for the group to follow single file down into the drainage ditch, not wanting to leave a large trail. Then about a foot step-up into the culvert. A young daughter began to cry. A mother quietly shushed her. The group slowly disappeared into the yawning darkness.

The entire day was bone-chilling cold. Seventy-six women and children lay huddled together with what blankets they had among them, on the concrete drainage floor. Sirens were heard. Some incredibly close. Some women had taken the liberty of placing duct tape on their youngest children's mouths. Every once in a while Jason could hear a baby whimper, but all in all, it was a quiet group. About noon, there was the sound of a dog, which sent chills up Jason's spine. Then it passed. People were cold and tired, mostly from the near starvation rations allowed by the guards. One bowl of rice per day. Another for every two children. The two mile trek to their underground hideaway had exhausted the group. They obviously needed proper shelter and food. Jason managed about 3 hours of interrupted sleep that day, but he himself was exhausted. At 5:30 pm, Jason stepped outside to see the end of what appeared to have been a dreary, miserable day. As if the weather agreed with him, it started to rain. Jason was second-guessing himself about not taking the hummer with him. If somehow he had been able to run the roadblock with a small group...but then what. No, the best he could hope for was to continue on the journey back home. It would be a cold, miserable trip. There was one small consolation, however. The clouds brought early darkness.

Protecting the prisoner had been a priority for Jason. Although he was disturbed about having to protect the guard from women he had undoubtedly molested, Jason's primary mission was to gather intelligence useful to Oak Ridge. When he told Destanee that the prisoner was not to be harmed, she became obviously upset. Apparently, Destanee had plans to eliminate the DHS agent the moment she had an opportunity. Jason had to explain that the prisoner had valuable information about where her husband was. After seeing her reaction, however, Jason decided to issue out rifles and pistols without magazines. Arming the group at this moment would only get everyone killed. The prisoner himself was weighed down with duffel bags which contained the grenades, extra ammunition, three radios, comsec, and intel. He could carry little more, especially barefooted and with his arms tied behind his back. The group moved on, walking down the gravel road in the light rain. Once, the group had to take cover in the ditch bank for what might have been a sheriff's car patrolling in the distance.

After two hours of walking, Jason had estimated they were about 5 miles away from Middleton. Children were crying; people were lagging behind. Now that everyone was soaked with rain, the weather had seen fit to change to sleet. Jason was shivering constantly. Quite honestly, considering the condition of the group, Jason did not know how the women and children could continue on. He knew the group must have been experiencing the onset of hypothermia. Up ahead there appeared to be a light. He signaled halt, but it was unnecessary. The group could not go on any farther. Following Jason's lead, the exhausted women and children managed to find a place under a small row of hedges, being half-frozen, huddling together. Jason himself continued on alone

The women waited, alone, cold. A half hour had passed. Another 15 minutes. No one stirred when the vehicle approached, the sound of a diesel engine growing loud. The group was bone cold, beyond tired and beyond concern. A tractor pulled up, with an old cotton trailer tarped over. The exhausted women and children gathered on the road, and the tarp was pulled back. Then one at a time, the group climbed up the ladder and dropped over the side, into a full batch of freshly-picked cotton.

At the farm ahead, Jason had talked to the farmer, who had been working in the cab of the tractor. He had hired three Mexican families to pick cotton this year, putting them up for the winter. In return, the men, their wives, and four children worked the farm, harvesting the cotton by hand. Negotiations had ensued. The farmer agreed to transport the group back to Bo Hill. In return, he would receive three rifles and two pistols plus ammunition. Jason did not like trading with weapons. One never knew when those weapons would be used against him and his family. Nevertheless, the group needed transport. Jason had no choice.

The weary group managed to keep warm in the harvested cotton under the plastic sheeting. Most of the group managed to shed their wet clothes, drying off in the bloom of soft warmth under the tarp. Three hours later, at the eastern roadblock of Pine View Road, near the Everling Farm, Jason was met by an armored Humvee with a top-mounted .50

caliber machine gun. It was Jeb and Tim, on patrol.

Jason and Mr. Wilson, a farmer about ten years Jason's senior, pulled up the drive to his home. Deborah rushed out and hugged her husband. He embraced his wife and explained how he had rescued a group of people who were still huddled in the trailer. Jason climbed the ladder and threw back the tarp. As cold and tired as he was, Jason managed total shock at what lay under the tarp. Out of the cotton began to emerge young women, almost all of them totally undressed. Realizing the humor of the moment as the naked women were being helped out of the container, Jason turned to Deborah. "They followed me home. Can I keep 'em?" Deborah had her hand on her hip and gave him the look.

The humor of the moment was lost again as the group was moved to the living room. The wood stove was stoked, and 76 people were huddled in that one room to warm up. People shared bowels, cups, and plates as hot oatmeal was handed out. The crowd's hunger seemed insatiable. Although the Hamilton's living room was considerably large, there was hardly any room to walk. Jason imagined the Bible story of Jesus feeding 5,000 people as empty bowls kept coming forward to be refilled. To Jason's knowledge, however, there was no miraculous replenishing of his own food stores, and soon they were out of oatmeal. The room grew warm between the people and the stove churning out heat, but it was a well-appreciated warmth.

Meanwhile, SSG Mosby had been radioed and asked if he could take in refugees. "Honestly, I do not know where to put them. I do have some MRE's here I can bring, but food is scarce. I thought this was a simple reconnaissance mission, Jason?"

"The world isn't very simple right now. Bo Hill, out."

At three a.m., the room was quieting down for the night. Jason undressed and lay down in his own bed with the love of his life in his arms. This moment was perfect, Jason realized. Actually the perfect moment only lasted about 30 seconds before Jason was sound asleep.

6 DHS AT BO HILL

Jason dreamed of being on a large boat and rescuing people drowning. In his dream he had realized there was a coming storm. When he awoke, he could only remember bits and pieces of it. It was daylight and tea kettles were whistling.

After a quick breakfast, Jason prepared to head to Oak Ridge. "A day earlier than planned," Jason thought. Arms and ammunition had been gathered and placed in the back of the truck: specifically six assault rifles, three pistols, and 35 full 20 round magazines of 5.56 and 150 rounds of 9mm, plus the frag grenades and the two AT4s from the back of the hummer in Middleton. He would take them into Oak Ridge along with the prisoner and gather information. Destanee would accompany them to verify or confirm any intelligence. The seventy-four refugees would be interviewed and filmed about the atrocities they had experienced or witnessed. So the plan was. Sometimes, however, things do not go as planned.

As he, Peter, and Philip were about to take off in the Sonoma, a shot. Then another. The sentry was signaling trouble on the north side of the highway. Already in the Sonoma and fully armed, Jason rode with his two sons across the front pasture to Bo Hill. About a quarter mile away, at the north barricade, was a hummer. DHS. Oh, my God! Jason thought. They had followed him home. Jason's heart raced as he ran into the house. The majority of Bo Hill were out of doors and running toward the hill within two minutes. 22 people had arrived, many of the new residents armed with their home defense shotguns that had been gifted to them. At the sentry point, they were traded in for assault rifles and grenades. In the treeline, trenches had been constructed on each side of the road, in the form of two Vs pointing north. These were manned as had been practice, half on each side of the road. Even forward of these, two men with AT-4s were deployed, designed to take out any vehicle assault. Machine gun teams would deploy to the west. All according to plan. All positions had been effectively concealed from the north with charcoal and dirt-soiled cloth. It was a decent defense considering Bo Hill had only 26 people. Jason hoped DHS had not brought air support.

Jason stepped forward into the road with SKS in hand. "What in the hell are you doing?" Deborah screamed adamantly as she ran toward him. "You cannot simply walk out there. You will be killed." Tears were in her eyes. Deborah went to her husband in the middle of the road, held him tightly, and whispered. "I just got you back. Please, don't go."

"I love you, Deborah," he whispered, kissing her neck as he held her. "But this has to be done."

Deborah cried something about her husband wanting to get himself killed, got in the Sonoma, and peeled gravel up Bo Hill toward their home. Jason knew his wife had a level head, even when upset. At least he told himself that as he made a steady pace on the highway toward the north barricade. At his left, invisible, the M60 team led by Officer Henry, was making its way through the woods.

It was clear DHS would ask questions; and it was also clear Jason could not simply let them leave. They had to be confronted.

Jason approached closer to the two hummers. The front hummer sported a top-mounted .50 caliber machine gun, enough firepower to turn Jason into a puddle. The thought was unnerving. Jason stopped within speaking distance, about a hundred feet away. Maybe 12 or 14 men in both of the vehicles.

"This is a government highway," the black-uniformed officer shouted as he dismounted the lead vehicle. The man continued in a patronizing tone. "How is it you see fit to block our road?"

"We do it to survive." Jason shouted back, still gripping his rifle. "Are you seeking permission to cross through?"

"We are the Federal Government. We need not ask permission from anyone."

The two men stared at each other.

"This land belongs to us, the people living here." Jason raised his hand and gestured, his face resolute "...And we will defend it. Lay down your arms, and you will not be harmed!"

Jason raised his hand and two large trees behind the vehicles fell, boxing them in. Jason heard the DHS gunner charge the .50 caliber. The officer, although rattled by Jason's display of courage, continued to speak.

"You sir, will drop your weapon and move forward, or you will be killed. You are now under arrest by the authority of the ..."

Jason dropped his right hand. A flash to the hummers' left was followed by a mighty boom which filled the air. The officer was no more to be recognized, having been assaulted with makeshift shrapnel. Officer Henry had placed a bullet through the gunner's throat, an unnecessary act as the gunner was also instantly killed by the explosion. The explosion echoed over the surrounding fields like a thousand shotgun blasts. The occupants of the first hummer, having had their driver evaporated in front of their eyes, and themselves directly in the way of a concussive explosion, were disoriented. The second hummer, without any mounted weapon, was still buttoned up. When the vehicle attempted to back up, over the branches and trunk of a rather large pine tree, it was faced with another vehicle driving in from its east flank. Jeb, who had been working patrol on Pine View Road in the hummer, pulled over the small ridge and stopped about 25 feet from the enemy combatants. Atop Jeb's hummer with .50 caliber gun at the ready, Juan looked ready to dish out destruction to all who resisted.

Jason had actually been knocked down by the force of the explosion. He could hear absolutely nothing. Slowly recovering, Jason walked the 100 feet between him and the DHS hummers, his ears still ringing and slightly bleeding. "Surrender or die," Jason shouted. Stunned agents opened up the doors, covered on both sides by three machine guns. Compliant, the 13 prisoners laid on the ground. Four of these prisoners were wearing the digital camouflage of the Army Combat Uniform. Although they were not wearing a unit patch on the side, Jason bet they were members of the 877th. "By the authority of the citizens of these United States and those of Bo Hill, I now place each of you under arrest...now does anyone have a roll of duct tape?"

The prisoners were to stay on the road. SSG Mosby had already sent out the HMETT and two other vehicles to transport some of the refugees. Questions needed answers. What was the tactical intent this DHS mission? Officer Henry searched the enemy prisoners thoroughly, logging down what was found on a small yellow notepad. When he searched the body of the officer who had been challenging Jason, he found some papers in a small satchel. "They appear to be on a probe mission of Oak Ridge. Orders were to engage any serious resistance. Apparently, they didn't reckon us to be serious."

Jason looked at the bloody remains of the officer's body. His unusually wry sense of humor could not be brought to bear. "They reckoned wrong," Jason replied matter-of-factly and turned back down the highway, walking home.

"Hey, Jason. Wait up," Officer Henry jogged after him. Catching up,

Henry commented. "You know you are a damned fool walking out there like that. How did you know that I had already placed those explosives? I mean, you were away."

"Honestly, Henry, I had forgotten about the explosives. And yeah, I feel like a selfish bastard, knowing about what was happening in Middleton and just ignoring it. Just don't mention me forgetting about the explosives to Deborah. She already thinks I have lost my mind." Jason walked on. He was exhausted.

Depressing the side switch on his Scooby Doo communicator, Jason signaled his two sons to come in relief. Both hummers appeared operational, although the paint and armored glass on the foremost hummer was thoroughly scoured by the C-4 blast. Turning the front hummer around, he positioned it on the two-lane highway with its gun trained on the prisoners, still laying face-down on the ground, devoid of equipment and ammunition, and arms. William and Peter had driven up in the black GMC Sonoma along with two shotgun-toting young women, who Jason did not immediately recognize. He nodded. Officer Henry took over the prisoner recovery operation while the M60 team and Jeb's hummer provided security to the north.

Jason took the Sonoma back. As he approached the defensive line of Bo Hill, he noticed people standing, much more than the twenty he had seen as he left. Deborah was standing at the top of the hill.

"I honestly debated whether to shoot you myself so I can stop having to worry about when it will happen. But, in any case, I thought we might use the extra help." Jason looked down at the trenches again. Women, armed with shotguns, hunting rifles, .22s, and pistols. A few were clutching nothing but a single hand grenade. "The three women who aren't here wanted to come as well, but someone had to watch the children." Jason held his wife, filled with so much emotion, not knowing whether to laugh or cry. He knew that Bo Hill had been lucky. No, that was the wrong word. It was obvious that someone had been watching over them.

The support vehicles from the reconstituted 877th had arrived from the south. Instead of transporting refugees for debriefing and interviews, it was agreed to transport prisoners. Officer Henry agreed to go back with them, since he was experienced in interrogation. When Jason walked with Officer Henry toward the pickup trucks, the ACU-clad civilian Soldiers saluted Jason, looking at him in awe. "Hell," Jason thought, "Do they not know the difference between an officer and a sergeant?" Jason walked up to the person in the HEMTT, who was apparently in charge of the convoy. "What's your name, Soldier?"

"Sergeant Bennet, sir."

"I am not a sir, but that's not important. Officer Henry is to assist SSG Mosby in interrogating these prisoners. He will be traveling back with you. Instruct your men not to allow communication of any kind among the prisoners. Kill anyone who disobeys. Do you understand?"

"Yes, sir," SGT Bennet answered smartly. Jason shook his head at the repeated mistake. "Sir, could I shake your hand. You *are* the one who saved our town, right?" Jason quietly shook his hand and walked off with Officer Henry.

"Henry, we simply cannot wait for DHS to find our weaknesses. We must be proactive. I cannot bear to think what would happened if DHS attacked Bo Hill in force, with air support. We need DHS command and control targets as well as supply targets. I would love to get these women's husbands back, and we need to find the 877th if they are still alive, but that does not take priority. Priority is the survival of Oak Ridge and Bo Hill. We need to buy some time.

"What is the plan regarding food and shelter for all these people?" Officer Henry put forth the question. "I don't think SSG Mosby could handle 80 more mouths to feed."

"As if we could. I will see if Robert is willing to part with more of that rice in his bins? Somehow, I think planting and protecting that corn this spring will become a major priority."

With Officer Henry leaving, Jason returned to his wife. "Love, these people might be at Bo Hill for a while. They have nothing. Their husbands are being held in Middleton. How much rice will these people need to last through the winter?"

"Well, honestly, hun, *we* have more than enough for our family to last for the rest of the year if we watch it. But that many people, that's ten times what we have here. We can't feed them; you know that."

This time it was Jason that gave Deborah the look. She thought for a moment. "They would need about 25 of those barrels for one year. Give or take. Or a little over two barrels per month."

"Thanks, baby. I love you.

"Oh, can you guess what we are eating for lunch today, by the way." Deborah placed her hand on her hip.

"Umm, rice?"

"Yes love, rice for everyone. Oh, those tin cans you insisted on keeping all this time? We needed dishes, so...." Somehow, even in this crazy time, Deborah's eyes managed to sparkle.

"You are beautiful, did you know that?" Deborah flashed her smile. "I know. Don't you forget that the next time you bring home a truckload of women." Jason wondered how his wife was able to manage all of the stress. The weight of all this added responsibility seemed to be crushing him.

In truth, simply surviving and post-traumatic stress were taking their toll on everyone. The cold weather as of late added to that burden. When

Jason was home, he seldom slept soundly, haunted by nightmares of death and loss. Deborah often woke up at night crying. Still, with everything that was happening around them, they both knew they were fortunate to have each other. Jason held his wife, not wanting to let go.

"Honey?" Deborah spoke softly in her husband's ear. "You *do* know what today is, right? ...Happy Thanksgiving. I love you." Jason silently thanked God for his family, realizing so many at Bo Hill did not have theirs with them.

After a while, Jason walked outside and talked with his oldest son. "William, I need your help. These women are going to be staying at Bo Hill, at least for a while. I am just too tired to deal with this right now. I got to get some rest. Can I count on you?"

"Sure, Dad. What do I do?"

"Well obviously, we can't house them at home here, but the houses on Ricker Road and the two by Church Creek are empty. Pick one volunteer for each house to go with you. That person can be the house leader. You need them settled in there as soon as you can."

"Do they have water nearby?"

"Son, I am going to let you think most of those things out. They need guns, too, if we can manage it. See Margarita and Deborah about food. Tim for blankets. Take everything from the shed, nothing from our pantry. Do you got this?

"I got this, Dad."

"Peter can help. He needs some time with his big brother."

* * *

The Northside Store

After a good night's rest, Jason decided it was time to visit Oak Ridge. SSG Mosby himself had been busy. He and his wife had been working with the owner of a local grocery store. Most groceries had long since been bought, but the store's owner had developed something of a barter system for business and trade. The Northside grocery store, which had also been a gun/ammo store, had been tenaciously defended by the owner and his family during the previous months. Now the store served as something of a town center, as it was the only retail establishment open in town. Here Mosby had been recruiting for the "Restored Independent 877th" to defend Oak Ridge. He and his wife were found distributing flyers explaining why Oak Ridge should remain free from federal control and federal "aid." In the last 2 days, Mosby had managed about 70 volunteers who were now under arms.

"Not exactly enough to defend a town, is it?" Mosby remarked as he and Jason stood talking on the parking lot, where a makeshift recruiting station was set up. "We are to have a town meeting tomorrow after the other two recons return."

"You know you can count on Bo Hill. We have about 26 under arms plus about 40 refugees who bore arms with us yesterday morning. But, yes, you do need more."

"Hey, are you the Master Sergeant who saved Oak Ridge."

Both men looked. It was a black teen, about 16, clad in an old battle dress uniform, a pair of sneakers, and a hoodie.

"Name is Jason, son." Jason offered his hand, and the youth accepted.

"Andre'. My brothers and I would like to help you, sir."

"How old are your brothers?"

"One is 19, and the other is 14."

"Why do you want to help?"

The tall young man looked at him with a face so earnest, there were almost tears in his eyes. "Sir, you are standing for something big. All my life, before this mess, I never stood for anything. You kept my hometown safe, my family safe. I want to do that."

Jason couldn't say no. "Well, you are a bit young, but welcome aboard."

"I won't let you down, sir."

Jason believed the youth. "And Andre', tell everyone there is to be a town meeting here at noon tomorrow."

Half of the guardsmen had been distributing flyers from door-to-door about the town meeting. "Come meet Master Sergeant Hamilton and SSG Mosby," the flyer read.

"I was happy to hear you made it back," Mosby remarked and grinned. "Otherwise, I would've had to make new flyers." By the end of the day, SSG Mosby had managed to enlist 30 more people into the Guard levy.

"We have sentries along Highway 1 and 14." Mosby spoke in the relative warmth of the HEMTT's cab. We also are manning Old Military Road. It is such a large area, I am wondering about response time.

"Mosby, they probably ain't coming in by vehicle, at least not at first. Probably by helicopter, and probably at night." This gave Mosby pause. "You know, they may have access to drones, too."

"What can we do against that?"

"What about Bartersville?"

"Well, as you know, Officer Henry came back with word from there two days ago. Twenty Guardsmen who refused to leave or acknowledge DHS authority were at the center. At that time, their arms room was intact, and he said they were going to move most military equipment to hiding. I have radio contact with them and a CEOI. There is, however, a significant gang presence in the town. Henry barely made it out of town alive. Didn't he mention that to you?"

"No, I guess he thought I had my own problems to deal with. Any word from higher?"

"Nothing from Camp Robinson. Command has been silent. There is talk from Jacksonport that the governor has been killed."

The two talked strategy. Where before, Homeland Security had been after the arms room and not expecting trouble, now they would come in force. Any traditional sentry would likely be an immediate target. In fact, going head-to-head against air assault troops sounded like suicide. There were no clear lines of battle, and such troops had the clear advantage of mobility. Jason had long thought about how to engage an enemy that is better equipped. The answer appeared to be misdirection.

"But what about the DHS helicopters?" SSG Mosby finally said, exasperated.

Jason thought for a moment, having an idea. "Just how many claymores do you have?"

* * *

Town Meeting

It was 1:00 a.m. Jason had made radio contact with Bo Hill. Although he would miss his Scooby Doo radios, the Singuars vehicle radios and handhelds were a bit superior. Juan, Destanee, and 6 other refugees would be at the courthouse at 8:00 p.m. The plan was to have these seven women speak at the town meeting about the injustices they had experienced and witnessed. Jason's flip-style video camera and two cell phones had been used to video several refugees at Bo Hill that afternoon as well. Anonymous flyers were to be published with photographs and testimonies about the atrocities committed by the federal government.

The other two recons returned at 1:30 a.m., pulling up at the armory in the dark blue truck. One of them, shot in the leg, had documented from several residents how the 877th Soldiers were being held at the county jail on the north side of Middleton. About a half mile away, the Riceland facility was tightly held by Homeland Security. He had sketches of guard positions and schedules for both places.

The other spy had reconned southwest Middleton. Here the middle class suburbs still clung to hope that there would be a recovery. Homeland Security patrols did not venture past the 63 bypass. Nor did DHS offer any relief when the riots of west Middleton had moved into their area. A militia of sorts had been formed along with a bitter taste for federal government interference. The leader? A retired Army Colonel named Miguel Fernandez, a naturalized citizen originally from the Philippines, had stood up against Homeland Security intervention, refusing to surrender his guns. As a result, the community of Valley View was being cut off, denied access to any food supplies. Could Fernandez be a possible ally?

It was 4 a.m. before Jason got some rest. Before then, copies of several interviews had been saved on computer. Volunteers were still transcribing hand-written testimonies of refugees and the recons on the computer so flyers could be printed. The next day, SSG Mosby would send out envoys to Bartersville, Jacksonport, Waynemont, Jacksonville Air Force Base, and the National Guard's Camp Robinson in Little Rock. Also, a recon would be sent to the state capital to see what was going on with the state government.

The wounded guardsman had been treated by Dr. Patel, a heart specialist who had lived out-of-state before the Meltdown had occurred. While operating, Dr. Patel explained nonstop to SSG Mosby what medical equipment was needed. Some sort of penicillin was necessary to treat this wound. He did not even have a needle and thread. He needed medical supplies. Just one more thing on the "to do list." Jason shivered, thinking what might happen if one of his son's needed serious medical treatment. Medical care was a priority as much as defense was.

At noon the next day, the parking lot was full. On one side, with a massive American Flag still waving behind them, stood most of the 877th Volunteers plus 20 people from Bo Hill, all with assault rifles. On the other was what looked to be almost a thousand people. No vehicles, though. Gasoline was scarce. SSG Mosby was manning the volunteer tent. Standing on a small platform, Jason introduced himself, and before he could finish, the crowd broke out in wild applause. Even with the bullhorn, it was difficult for him to be heard. Jason introduced the seven refugees, all women, who had prepared notes from which they read. It was explained how families had been kidnapped and forced into labor. The entire crowd was shocked when one woman described how a senior DHS officer had executed her six-year-old son, shooting him in the head in front of her and others. Others recalled similar events, where people who refused to cooperate with DHS searches were summarily executed. Then the two recons from Oak Hill also testified of their findings, testimonies of cruelty and brute force, documented both by video and sworn statements.

When the one militia recon reported about the 877th, there was a murmur in the crowd. These Soldiers were people they knew, family members. Imprisoned. Reports of torture. Someone cried out an expletive that DHS agents should be hunted down. The crowd was rightfully angry.

Then Jason took the bullhorn. He had prepared words, but he folded the paper and put it into his jacket pocket.

"I understand how you feel. I love America." Jason paused. "But anyone government who starves, rapes, and murders it citizens, they are not America. America is pure. Many men have died to keep America that way. And so have the good men of Oak Ridge."

"Now I am a law-abiding citizen. I've worked hard to feed my family. I have prayed to God more in these last two months than I ever did when I went to church. And *by* God, I will defend my family. And I will defend my land. Now this..." the PA squealed as Jason moved his arm around the packed parking lot. "These are your families. And, by God, this is your land! The question is 'Will you stand with us now in our time of need?'"

It was a question, not a speech. Jason did not expect the response. The crowd erupted in cheers and applause. The lines for volunteers filled. By 3:00 p.m., more than 400 people had volunteered to join the 877th. In reality, everyone had, in effect, volunteered to make Oak Ridge work. And there was immediate work to be completed. Defense lines needed to be dug. Training and drills needed to occur.

There were other needs in Oak Ridge as well. The storeowners, a Mr. Holloway and his wife, agreed to support an outreach to the local farmers. Reestablishing local trade was important if Oak Ridge was ever to recover from this disaster. There was food still out there on the farms that simply needed access to the market. Oak Ridge still needed a police department and judge. Officer Henry expressed interest in reforming the police department. Henry had a heart for law and justice.

The local mayor had shown up at the meeting, an unsavory sort of man. He had not spoken at the event as if he didn't want to take sides. It was as if he were waiting to see which way the political wind would blow. Jason had doubted that the mayor was a man of character the moment he laid eyes on him. Nevertheless, the mayor was allowed to swear in Officer Henry as Police Chief of Oak Ridge. It looked as if Jason would be losing a neighbor.

* * *

The First Battle of Oak Ridge

It was seven days later, on a Sunday night, when DHS forces hit, and they hit hard. Without warning, two helicopters strafed well-lit sentry posts on Highway 1, next to the closed Mexican restaurant and 18 troops repelled in north of the position, with orders to secure the highway. One lone sentry seemed frightened and ran off into a drainage ditch, dodging the DHS gunfire as he ran. He finally disappeared among a group of houses near the railroad tracks. Gunpowder and silence hung in the air as the DHS members moved by team toward the highway guard post.

Across town at the National Guard armory, members of the reconstituted 877th nervously waited under canvas in the cold of night, unmoving when they heard the distant gunfire. During the previous week, fighting positions with interlocking fields of fire had been constructed and explosive charges were planted, however in a direction opposite of what logic might dictate. Guns were pointed downhill, into the National Guard compound rather than away from it. A handful of brave volunteers manned the guard posts within the Guard center, inside foxholes dug perhaps a bit too deep into the earth.

The helicopters swept over the ridge in the dark of night and strafed the well-lit center's sentry position at the Guard Center gate. The pilots

Tuesday Meltdown

were unaware that the vast number of men was directly below them at the edge of the perimeter. Also unknown was the fact that the entire guard center inventory had been moved to the old jail complex downtown. SSG Mosby and Jason had turned the entire guard center into a bright, shiny fishing lure. They were fishing for the Department of Homeland Security and had just got a huge bite.

The sodium vapor spotlights lit up the sky more than lighting the ground. Although the lighting was a bit odd, the chopper pilots didn't seem to notice as they strafed the sentry positions with .50 caliber tracer rounds, ripping up earth. The Guard sentries were beaten down, overwhelmed. Moving in, 4 helicopters dropped approximately 40 black-clad DHS agents into the perimeter of the compound.

Suddenly, where there had once been bright yellow lights, came the brilliant flash-booms of explosions. Claymore mines had been mounted directly under the floodlights on the wooden light poles themselves. The explosions left little of the light poles, splintering them. Thousands of small steel balls were exploded in midair causing even more destructive results. One helicopter immediately burst into flame, penetrated by 2000 pieces of steel shot. Another helicopter was forced to set down. A hail of gunfire assaulted the downed aircraft and the 40 DHS agents. Surprisingly, the sentries who had taken cover, popped up to return fire upon the would-be invaders, supported by over one hundred and fifty members of the 877th.

Another explosion burst overhead, and sparks flew from another chopper's engine. A contrail of smoke marked the rocket from an AT4, which pointed like a finger to a fireball enveloping the disabled aircraft. It crashed into a group of pines about 10 yards from a foxhole, and the fuel tank erupted into a boom that echoed against the hillside and over the entire town.

The final helicopter began strafing the 877th's northern hillside perimeter with its side-mounted M60. An air horn sounded, barely audible above the gunfire. With that signal, the entire north perimeter lifted up rifles together, forming a deadly wall of lead assaulting the remaining Blackhawk. The 877th's eastern flank joined in, causing the final bird to spin wildly. The chopper appeared to recover as it went over the hill into darkness. Then a bright light and explosion.

Below, the remaining DHS agents were not going quietly. SSG Mosby pulled out a bullhorn from the hilltop. "Hold your fire! Hold your fire! The popcorn like gunshots slowly died. "This is SSG Mosby of the reconstituted 877th Engineering Battalion." We have taken out your air support. You are completely surrounded. There are 3 claymore mines covering your locations. If you do not surrender immediately, we will respond with overwhelming deadly force." In truth, SSG Mosby had no more claymores set up, but the bluff achieved results.

Quiet, then a shout. "We are coming out." 13 DHS agents, some wounded, managed to make their way into the light, hands held high.

The battle occurring on Highway 1 was another story. Two helicopters were providing air support for the 18 air assault troops who had repelled in about 100 yards north of the sentry post. Unknown to DHS, Oak Ridge militia had dug in about twenty yards to the front of the actual sentry post. These positions were camouflaged with hay, concealing the positions well among the surrounding dead grass. One DHS agent actually walked on top of a covered positions as his team moved quickly toward the empty sentry post. The agents were receiving fire to their front from militia sniping them with hunting rifles. The snipers were having a tough go at it, however, as the helicopter pilots with night vision were constantly engaging their position. About when the agents had made the guard shack, a tremendous gasoline explosion disentegrated the shack. The hidden militia popped the coverings of their concealed positions and fired into the rear flank of the advancing invaders. Half of the agents were immediately dropped in the surprise move. The remaining DHS agents took cover on both sides of the highway, being assaulted with crossfire. The helicopters continued air support, strafing the newly revealed positions, but they were hampered by automatic small arms fire. Even after the Blackhawks broke off, the remaining agents would continue to hold out until after daylight, doggedly refusing to surrender. In the daylight, the agents were easy pickings for militia marksmen. The agents died to a man in barren cotton fields cloaked with a fresh white: the first snow of the season.

SSG Mosby's first thought was to pursue the enemy and destroy them. Jason had to calm him down, reminding him that only two helicopters had escaped and they had had remarkable success considering Alpha Company had no air support. Better to tend to the unit's wounded and maintenance, maintain an over-watch, and gather information.

The casualties of this first Battle of Oak Ridge were relatively modest for a town racked with hardship. Before today, eighty-four deaths had been reported in the town, yet there were almost two hundred people missing. Some dead had only been discovered last week during the door-to-door outreach and militia levy. A nursing home on the edge of town had contained 12 bodies, all of which appeared to have died of dehydration. The body of one elderly man had been found hanging over a dry toilet. Uncontrolled looting and crimes associated with it on the south side of town had also been a contributing factor to the body count. Diabetes and other medical conditions had taken their own toll. Oak Ridge was already familiar with hardship. So the first Battle of Oak Ridge was little more than a bad day for its citizens.

In all, 22 guardsmen and 10 militia had been killed. Most of them were the result of aircraft strafing. There were 21 wounded with 6 mortally so. One of the wounded had been saved only by the quick thinking of his battle buddies. His lower left leg had been literally shot off by 7.62 mm machine gun rounds. His buddies had managed to stop the bleeding using a tourniquet and a propane torch.

There was one nurse, an experienced veteran nurse who had worked trauma at the same hospital Jason's wife had worked. She was making rounds, doing the work of a doctor. Doctor Patel did the work of God. He would not sleep for the next 25 hours, and had actually saved three of those thought mortally wounded. "I could have saved more had I had proper supplies. I am working with a sewing kit and hardly any anesthesia here."

Jason and Mosby walked the two blocks from the old jail to the county courthouse. The battle the night before and the aftermath the next day had made for a long day. It was, however, beautiful as the sunlight shone golden over the light dusting of snow, both of which painted the empty streets and buildings with a rich magic. With the two walked the mayor, a slick, thin-framed salesman of a man. When Jason had first shook the mayor's hand, he had taken note the mayor's limp handshake and his toothy smile. Both Jason and Mosby agreed Oak Ridge deserved a better mayor. Mayor Harris was dirty to the core. He was, however, mayor, and the Oak Ridge government needed all of the legitimacy it could get.

The twelve captured DHS agents were being held in the Wilson County Courthouse. Two prisoners had died from injuries. The others had been attended to. Entering in through the eastern door, the only door with the glass still intact, Jason noted the piles of glass and plaster swept up on the floor. Slowly but surely the town of Oak Ridge was cleaning up. Although the courthouse had been looted, the basement rooms were still strong, making for great holding cells. Descending the steps was like descending in time to a simpler era, or perhaps better said, an earlier time. Rich mahogany handrails and steps deceptively led to a narrow gray hall lined with strong metal doors.

"Who are you going to talk to?"

"No idea," Jason replied matter-of-factly. Jason wished to himself that Officer Henry were here. In fact the new Chief of Police, along with his twelve new police officers, were patrolling the streets. The door was opened, and Jason walked inside. One of the first things that Jason insisted on was that the prisoners not be allowed to communicate with each other. In fact, the prisoners had been placed in twelve separate rooms in the basement and first floor. "Silence, segregate, and speed" had been the military mantra he followed to ensure prisoners did not collaborate on any misinformation or escape plans. Now he walked into the first room, its heavy metal door creaking open. The oil lamp carried by Mosby cut into the darkness and into the prisoner's face.

"What right have you to keep me here!"

"What right do you have to attack our town?"

"You are the same as those backwater hicks from the National Guard. They refused to obey the President's executive orders." The smug toothy smile from the prisoner was arrogant. "Your treacherous actions have condemned this entire town. Did you ever think you could win against the United States of America?"

"Oh, you mean the way we kicked your ass yesterday? And if you think a government that can treat its citizens this way is the United States of America, I got news for you. You are on the wrong side." And with that, Jason abruptly left, angry.

Closing the door, Jason remarked to Mosby "Well, that was pointless." Jason watched as the mayor walked back upstairs. Then Jason confided to Mosby quietly, "I don't trust the mayor." "We must rescue the 877th. We need to rescue them soon, and hit hard."

7 CHRISTMAS RESCUES

It was only ten days later, but winter had definitely arrived. One did not need the Weather Channel to understand that a massive arctic high had swept into the United States and had turned everything into a mess of winter precipitation. In Arkansas, that meant freezing rain, sleet, and ice. Only the desperate would dare go out in such dangerous conditions. The people of Oak Ridge and Bo Hill were that desperate.

During these last 10 days, Jason had coordinated with Colonel Fernandez in Valley View. Colonel Fernandez had been an Army dentist. When Jason spoke with him, Fernandez confided that he had absolutely no combat experience. He had simply refused to give away his only means to defend his family. Refused to be bullied. As a ranking member of the Veteran's of Foreign Wars, he was among those that decided Valley View would defend its community. They had stood up against the North Middleton riots and the ensuing jail escape. Now they were attempting to stand their ground against Homeland Security, who wanted to strip all their constitutional rights in exchange for a bowl of rice. A joint outreach to farmers southwest of Middleton had provided some needed relief for the people of Valley View. Three farmers had shared wheat and rice in exchange for a promise of security and trade.

During that time, the envoy Oak Ridge sent to Jacksonport had also returned. According to his report, Jacksonport had been devastated by looting. Hundreds of people, who had lived their entire lives dependent on the government, were now unable to provide for themselves. Their sense of entitlement produced an outrage the very first day their food stamps failed. Stores were looted. Police were overwhelmed. The National Guard, under a state of national emergency, was activated. For three days, an indecisive lieutenant colonel had sat on his hands, following explicit orders to do nothing while most of the town burned. On the evening of the third day, the command sergeant major, a 30-year weathered combat veteran, relieved the colonel of his command. Force had been used to restore order, and a curfew was in effect. Their was no federal relief, but Homeland Security did send a rather arrogant agent to "take charge" of the scene. The sergeant major had sent him back on his way toward Middleton like a brat who had received his first spanking.

It was this person that the envoy had spoken with, a Sergeant Major Roland. The sergeant major had watched the videos regarding federal atrocities, read the testimonies, and was outraged at the federal government's conduct. The veteran soldier, however, found himself undermanned, attempting to provide law enforcement for a starving city. Radio communications between Jacksonport and Oak Ridge had been coordinated and established. There was little the sergeant major could do to help at the moment, but he sympathized with Oak Ridges's plight.

Now, with two inches of solid ice on the roads of Oak Ridge, even 4-wheel drive vehicles had to inch their way forward, making movement near impossible. But not totally impossible. At midnight, six large farm tractors were transporting militia of the Reconstituted 877th and Bo Hill in cotton trailers. At 3:30 a.m., in near zero visibility, the convoy pulled through the sleepy town of Bennett, crossed the railroad tracks, and started up the hill on Duncan Road. The tractors' tires provided traction where no other vehicle could dare travel. After an hour, the convoy was within ½ mile of Stone County Sheriff's Department and Detention Center. Jason and Jeb approached on foot cautiously, climbing a pile of stacked electric poles, located on a ridge to the north of the facility. Together, they viewed the jailhouse: three large buildings joined together by a lower brick office-like entrance. The entire facility was surrounded by a 14-foot chain link fence topped with two rolling strands of concertina wire.

"Looks more like a prison than a jail," Jeb said.

"That facility can hold 470 prisoners." Jason answered. "There is an electronic board located next to the containment room that can unlock any and all cells."

"How much resistance do you expect again?"

"Intel said three hummers moved in and out during shift change. Can't be more than eighteen."

"I hope for your sake, intel is right. That place seems huge."

"They must be running a skeleton shift. God knows how they can feed that many prisoners with so few people. There. That is new." Jason pointed to a wooden guard tower that had been erected. Inside, there appeared to be two guards, although he couldn't be sure.

The cold beads of sleet whipped across Jason's face as he sat studying the complex below him. Further off, he could see the Riceland facility, its three largest grain elevators being the highest structures in the city. There lay the real threat. Tracked vehicles and possible air support from there would be the death knell for any escape plan. There could not be any outside explosions. The tower must be taken out by limited small arms. It had to be quick and quiet; otherwise, a response force from the nearby DHS would spell disaster. The cold was so bitter that Jason's fingernails began to hurt even under his gloves. It was time.

At approximately 5:30 a.m., three DHS hummers reported a disturbance on Jackson Avenue, near the local university campus. Molotov cocktails were thrown, and a roadblock had been created. It was obvious to Homeland Security, whose headquarters were at the Riceland facility, that it was civilian rioting. Three tracked vehicles would be deployed, no need for air coverage, especially in this weather.

A minute prior to this attack, three DHS hummers had pulled up to the jail complex and pushed the button at the facility's main gate. They would be about 10 minutes earlier than usual that morning, nothing out of the ordinary, considering the weather. A buzzer sound was heard and the tall chain link gate slid out of the way. Bundled up for winter weather, the relief entered the lobby and faced the desk clerk, who was behind impact-resistant glass.

Not recognizing the relief, the desk clerk looked concerned, asking if the dark-clad men were new. Andre' smiled and approached the counter, looking a bit young for a guard. "I guess you could say that." He pulled the pin of a grenade, slipped it into the metal tray, pushed it closed, and hit the floor. The explosion immediately killed the desk clerk and his partner. Jason ran up with a half-block of C4 and placed it up to the entry door. Andre' and Jason moved back outside where 13 other men waited. A concussive blast, contained somewhat by the jail's lobby, shattered the glass doors of the entrance way as well as the impact resistant glass of the front office. Jason, William, and seven others went through the entry door while Andre' took his team through the administrative office. The potshots of small arms fire filled the chambers of the jailhouse. Two guards were to the immediate front of Jason, but the narrow hallway did not lend itself to cover. Jason fired a three-round burst from his 9mm carbine, striking the first of the guards in the chest with two of the shots. Jason directed a second burst toward the second guard, while the remaining guard returned fire. The final guard dropped as Jason felt a sharp impact of a round hitting his leg. Could he move forward, yes. But it began to burn like hell. Move forward. No prisoners; there was no time.

In the lone watchtower, two guards, confused by what was occurring below them, were scanning the perimeter using high-powered rifles. There was nothing for them to shoot at. Suddenly three militia in the dark tree line began firing upon the tower using scoped hunting rifles.

Now the muffled shots inside the complex were matched by a small shootout between the tower and militia marksmen. It quickly became evident that the outside shooting match was one-sided. One militia man fell over dead, shot cleanly in the head. The tower guards had night vision scopes. Another militia sniper fell. Underneath the tower, someone began making his way up the narrow wooden stairs to the top. Opening the small metal hatch, William popped up with a 9mm carbine, shooting one tower marksman in the chest. The agent was knocked back, his vest taking the impact. The other guard turned toward him with the long barrel of the rifle, but William was quicker, bringing his shorter weapon to bear and squeezed off three rounds. One shot hit the second guard in the face. The first guard, recovering, had pulled his pistol. Both he and William fired at the same time. William hit the remaining guard in the neck, a quick kill. The guard, however, had also hit his target.

Inside the jail, the fight was over. Five jail guards had chosen to fight and die. Six remaining officers had surrendered and were being held in the front office.

One obviously nervous guard was escorted to the limited area's control panel. "You are going to open all of the cells." Jason announced then he walked into the main holding area. "We are looking for the members of the 877th. Slowly, uniformed men, no shells of men, thin and frail from the effects of starvation, emerged from cells.

"We need those tractors down here now, Jeb!" Jason shouted on his radio, the pain in his leg almost unbearable.

"Master Sergeant!"

Jason turned around to see his oldest son being helped along by two men. William's wound had been bandaged, but the young man was on the edge of consciousness. Painfully limping toward his son, Jason listened as William managed "I did it, Dad. I took the tower."

"You did well, son," Jason spoke softly, tears in his eyes. Then William passed out.

Jason looked up to see a tall, gaunt skeleton of a man. How the man managed to even hold himself up was a miracle. Then recognition. SSG Moses? "Moses, where is everyone else? I mean a battalion has more than this, right? SSG Moses's sad eyes communicated more than words. "Seventy-four present for duty, Master Sergeant. 273 dead, and eighteen traitorous bastards," SSG Moses spoke bitterly.

"A Team, give these men a weapon, if they can carry one. I need pictures of these men for documentation. Johnson, Peters, wounded go in the front hummer with me. B team, security sweep of the area for weapons and ammo. Jail the guards. Pickup in 5 minutes."

The shock of losing almost 300 men echoed in Jason's mind. His oldest son injured added to that shock. Then an interruption. It was the B-team leader. "Sir, you need to look at this." The pain in Jason's calf had somehow shot up his entire left side. Jason leaned against the wall and slowly pushed himself forward into a side room. Inside the room was a barber's chair but with disturbing modifications. Straps were present to secure a person's wrists, feet, and neck. And to the side, pliers, box cutters, and various tools covered in blood. This was not what the team leader was pointing toward. In a wastebasket were what appeared to be body parts: teeth, fingernails, and three fingers. And beside that wastebasket, a man huddled, naked and cowering, with his arms covering his head. Oh my God, Jason thought.

"Sir, we're here to help," Jason told him, removing his gortex jacket to cover the man. "It's going to be okay. Who are you?"

"I am... 1st Lieutenant Michael Ryan of the 877th," the man cried out. Whether it was the pain, the shock, or what he had just witnessed, Jason felt the room swimming. He slapped his palm against his wounded leg to keep from passing out and screamed.

"Change of plans." Jason managed. "The guards are coming with us. Those sick sons-of-bitches are going to answer for the twisted things they have done." "Get out your camera," Jason instructed the B team leader. "Get all of this." Then Jason passed out.

Andre' and the team leader used a two-man carry to get Jason on the table. "Get me a field dressing!" the team leader yelled.

The 7 remaining members of the support team, led by Jeb had arrived and the 877th were slowly loaded on board. Jeb decided to take another 10 minutes and load up an empty trailer with food provisions and bedding, things the current occupants of the jail had seen little of. Cases upon cases of canned fruit, dried milk, vegetables, pasta, sugar, coffee, soups, and canned spam were found. Then came army issue wool blankets and pillows. Although visibility was limited, there was a direct line of sight the half-mile separating the jail from DHS headquarters. It would be light soon. They had to move.

"Morning light in 31 minutes. We move out now, Jeb commanded."

The convoy moved forward with Jeb in the lead vehicle along with Jason and his son, both wounded. Following him were the tractors, then one hummer convoying in dawn's early light. The other hummer stayed back to rendezvous with Colonel Fernandez and his 4 volunteers, who had created the diversion at the university campus.

Jason awoke some three hours later as the convoy was arriving in Oak Ridge. Like the cold morning sunshine, the battle had been bitter sweet. Three militia had been killed; three wounded including himself and his son. Seventy-two other soldiers, some unable to walk, having been starved and tortured, were in the trailers behind them. Much fewer survivors than had been expected, and in much worse condition. Jason could not wrap his mind around what he had seen in the jail. Could the guardsmen have been rescued any sooner? Although Oak Ridge would view this as a victory, Jason could feel none of it as he held his wounded son in his arms.

Pulling past a small wooden church, Jason looked ahead at the highway. Jeb drove a steady 15 miles an hour over the ice, not daring to go any faster. Across from Jason, Andre' was applying pressure to William's wounded left shoulder. Behind him, another militia man was holding his left hand with his right. He had lost two fingers. Three other men in the back of the vehicle had lost their lives. SSG Moses rode shotgun in the front seat, gently nursing a can of evaporated milk. The Staff Sergeant's sad, tired eyes caught onto something up ahead. Jason looked ahead and noticed it as well. It was the huge American flag, still proudly on display at the edge of town. There was something else flying above the flag. A red cloth? Below, the sentry stood. Lanterns and Christmas wreaths surrounded the post. As the convoy pulled up, a lone sentry saluted. A sign was painted in red on a large white sheet. "This We Will Defend."

* * *

Recovery at Bo Hill

The month of December was relatively quiet. At Bo Hill, plans were being drawn up for liberating the refugees' husbands, but quite honestly, surviving the especially harsh winter was enough challenge for everyone. Rations of rice were issued, but everyone was at work collecting food and firewood when it was warm enough go outside.

William had been transported home with Jason after Dr. Patel had stitched him and his father up, pumping them both full of antibiotics. Rest, fluids, and keep the wounds clean. They should both make it if infection did not set in. In the movies, being shot is a flinch and a wince where, later, the good guy walks away with the girl, holding his injured arm. In reality, most gunshots kill unless the bleeding can be stopped. Even then, it is a nasty hole that makes one feel as if he had been hit by a freight train for weeks afterward. Tamera worried over William, constantly bringing him soups, and holding their daughter Savannah where both could visit. Savannah was growing up quite well, standing up on her own and able to climb on and off the couch. It was hard to believe she would be one-year-old at the end of the month.

Jason used the time of his recovery to show off one of his less redemptive qualities: impatience. Jason had been unable to move for a solid week, as his body reacted to the severe trauma of having a nine-millimeter bullet pass through its muscle tissue. He simply had to lie still, and it was literally driving him insane. At nights, Jason had nightmares of his family being murdered or tortured. During the day, he felt the need to constantly worry about the food situation, defenses, the weather, and everything else. He was constantly tossing, turning, and, quite honestly, bothering everyone in the house. Once, three days after Jason's return home, there had been a muster at the hill. At the end of the muster, Jason could not be found in his bed. Following a trail of vomit and blood out to the front pasture, however, Deborah found Jason easily enough, unconscious, passed out from the pain. In his hands, his SKS. The muster had been a false alarm; someone had shot a deer.

That evening, Jason seemed to remember seeing Deborah. It could have been a dream; everything seemed hazy. His wife kissed him on the forehead, and told him not to worry. "God has all of this under control. Who do you think saved your butt all this time, you silly idiot." Then she stuck his arm with something, and he slept soundly. Over the next week, the swelling and redness in Jason's leg reduced, better revealing the massive hole of the exit wound. Jason had a hole the size of a poker chip in his left calf.

Time had passed. Jason did not know how long it had been, but he was determined to get up. He sat up and began the process of getting dressed. Almost an hour later, he struggled with his boots. Deborah had seen him. She didn't offer to help Jason, but she didn't stop him either. She had radioed Dr. Patel ten days ago, fearful for her husband's life. The medication the doctor prescribed had managed to slow Jason down, allowing him to recover. Pulling his second boot on, Jason duly received his wife's comment with a painful groan: "If you fall and kill yourself, don't say I didn't tell you so." Peter and Philip were in the woods, trapping birds, and Jason wanted to be with his sons.

At Bo Hill and pretty much everywhere else, meat was getting to be a luxury. Everyone understood that the 6 goats and 5 remaining sheep should be spared this winter unless there was an emergency. The sheep and goat herds needed to be built up, saved, and traded. The rams and billies had already been tupping, and hopefully this early spring would be a literal time of rebirth. From the domestic rabbits, a pair had been given to each refugee house. This had reduced Jason's number of rabbits to 24. No more rabbits for meat on Saturdays. The same with chickens. Eggs were to be hatched to expand the livestock. If Jason's family could survive this winter without thinning their supply of livestock, it might mean there would be enough for next year.

Sparing the livestock this year meant hunting and trapping. Possums, rabbits, squirrels, and raccoons were occasionally trapped, snared, and shot along Church Creek and Big Creek. Last week, Tim had dropped a deer with an AR15. With about 100 people living there, however, game around Bo Hill was getting scarce. Anything, including small birds, was quite literally fair game. The old lyrics "Four and twenty blackbirds baked in a pie" had come to life when Margarita had shown both Maria and Deborah how to remove the thumbnail sized pieces of breast meat from the small fowl. "Boil 'em first, then pluck and pull," she had reminded the ladies in a thick Mexican accent.

Jason had managed to make it to where Peter and Philip were trapping on the wooded acreage south of their home. "Dad, watch this," Peter said quietly. In front of them was a sea of blackbirds, covering the shore around the small frozen pond. "See, it only takes a few seconds." The boys baited their trap with rice and breadcrumbs. "There must be 6 birds in there again, and I just cleared the trap 10 minutes before. It's crazy."

Peter pulled the string, trapping the birds under the box. He then picked up the box, being careful not to open the bottom, and shook it rigorously. Inside Jason could hear the birds hitting the box. Then Peter opened the box and poured the dizzy birds on the ground. Philip was ready with a 1"x4" board, clubbing the defenseless creatures.

Jason knew it took more than 24 blackbirds to make a meal for his family. Still, he was amazed at how Peter had devised an effective trap. "Son, could you use a net to catch them? I think I have a badminton net in the shed." Philip ran back to get the net. Within two hours, Philip and Peter had netted over 100 blackbirds. Of course, that meant one thing left to do. The boys had to clean them. Although in pain, the sunshine and opportunity to be with his children was good medicine for Jason. He found himself content plucking feathers and pulling breast meat with his sons. His family needed more days like this.

Where meat was scarce, luxuries such as coffee, sugar, and chocolate were even more so. At the market in Oak Ridge, the going rate for sugar was twice the weight in meat. Chocolate bars were even more expensive. One day Juan had come back excited. He had managed to trade 20 pounds of venison for 4 pounds of sugar and *two* cans of cocoa. Maria would make him a Christmas cake.

It was indeed Christmas. Tim had taken up a project out in the shed. When Jason had painfully managed to make his way out to visit, Tim welcomed him in and invited him to try a drink. What Jason tasted was something like vodka except for much stronger and with a slight lactic aftertaste.

Tim grinned. "Made it with this." Tim pointed to a 25 gallon metal keg with a fire underneath. "Gotta keep the fire going the right way. Too much, and you lose your steam. Too little doesn't work. Keep the top sealed." Then, he pointed to the copper tubing. "It goes to this keg and comes out here. Now see this." He pointed to a third keg. "This works best right now because you can put ice in the water to cool it." Out of that keg's side was the copper tubing's end. A tiny stream of clear liquid was falling into a mason jar.

"I can make 20 quarts of mash from 10 quarts of rice and some yeast. That makes 7 jars of shine. In other words, I can make 5 times my trade back at the store." It was true, they did have enough rice. It seemed that

Bo Hill would make it through the winter, now that Robert had helped out with the extra rice.

"And ya can feed mash to the goats afterward. Fun to watch those little animals fall over." Tim was grinning ear to ear.

"What the hell," Jason gave in to another sip. "Hey, I bet we could make this smoother and lighter if we used a charcoal filter. Can you do this with corn?" Jason limped stiffly up the hill back toward the house. "Oh, Tim," Jason called back, "Don't give too much mash to those poor goats." Jason grinned and walked inside.

* * *

Christmas Day

With two days before Christmas, both Jason and Juan had been canvasing the neighborhood of Highfield, which was about a mile away from Bo Hill. More often than not, they were met with rifles pointed at them. It was only when Jason, who was using a cane, introduced himself that the ice began to break. The most frequent question they were asked after that was something along the lines of "Are you that Master Sergeant guy who rescued the 877th?" Jason attempted to explain that there were many people involved. He was asking for support for a neighborhood patrol and support for the security checkpoints at Highway 1 and 167. In return Bo Hill offered garden seed, plot space for tending corn, and trade with both Oak Ridge and Bo Hill. The idea of knowing and looking out for neighbors appealed to those living along the ridge road and those on the west side of the ridge. Some homesteads were self-sustaining. Other homes were barely getting by and jumped at the chance to grow food. The back of the truck also had 5 gallon buckets of rice for those in need. After all, it was Christmas.

And so it was that the Hamiltons obtained a boyfriend for their boxer, Bailey. A poverty-stricken family in Highfield had little to feed their children, much less their dog. The young man, Justin Davenport, listened to Jason speak and agreed with the idea of resisting the federal government's tyranny. With a thick Australian accent, he explained how he had moved into this empty trailer in October after escaping from Middleton. In Middleton, he and his family had suffered under the rule of thugs, all unofficially sanctioned by DHS. Indeed, after someone had signed up for public assistance, it was now illegal for that person to change residence without approval. As he told his story, Jason realized just how much the young man had experienced this year, watching him tense up with latent hostility. Justin told his desire to fight, to stand up and do something. Yet, he explained with tears in his eyes, that he was having problems simply feeding his family, and was even considering slaughtering his dog. As if the dog had heard his name, the big boxer lifted himself off the floor, trotted to the door, and pushed its head next to his master's leg. Justin's two small boys poked their heads into the daylight as well. Jason lifted out two 5-gallon containers of rice from the back of the Sonoma. The young man was speechless. Jason put his hand on the young man's shoulder. "It is going to be okay, son," Jason told him. "Your family is going to make it. We are here for you. Merry Christmas."

"Merry Christmas," the man finally managed to say, tears of gratitude in his eyes. "I will not forget this, sir." Somehow, Jason had ended up with the dog.

It was warm for a Christmas Eve Day, and quiet. The midday sun had melted the last bit of ice and thawed the ground, making it mushy. Jason and Deborah were out on the front porch in their chairs, holding hands. Their dogs Bailey and Chief sat in front of them, also soaking up the warm afternoon. It could have been an ordinary day if it were not for the two rifles propped up beside them. Inside, Deborah had her Christmas tree. Philip had picked it out, cut it, and brought it in. Where it might not have been the ideal store purchase for any other Christmas, it was the perfect Christmas tree this year, lifting everyone's spirits. The entire house, which before had been reduced to a sparse, utilitarian décor of necessity, was now traped in garland, ribbons, and ornaments, all celebrating the love God had shown humanity two millennia before. Christmas was a time to celebrate.

It was Deborah's idea to go caroling, but everyone was quick to get involved. Although Jason couldn't walk very well, he insisted on caroling with his family. The result of this was Jason and William, who were recovering remarkably well, being loaded in the back of the Sonoma along with gifts. The refugees at Ricker Road and Church Creek were flooded with gifts, mostly useful items such as canned goods, pots, blankets, and Mason jars. Officer Henry came with his family; Jeb and Nora came with theirs. Juan and Maria had their baby with them walking behind the procession, looking like the holy couple of that first Christmas Eve night. Children's eyes lit up as chocolate fudge was handed out. Somehow, Robert, who had gotten wind of the entire affair, arrived with his wife Sue and was passing out popcorn balls. Even Tim, at Haley's prodding, was caught up in the spirit of the season, and handed out pint jars of his ever-improving distilled product. It was Christmas, after all, and, although the carolers were packing enough firepower to fight a small war, that night they were wishing everyone peace on earth and good will toward all men.

Oak Ridge had experienced a recovery of its own during the month of December. The 72 guardsmen were in better health, although many had nightmares of the torture they had been through. SSG Moses's wife somehow received word that her husband was back, and she was living in Oak Ridge now. Justice was also being dealt out in the town of Oak Ridge, as well. Six Middleton jail guards were brought to trial for specific acts of torture and inhumane cruelty. Forty-six witnesses of the 877th testified of horrible, unspeakable acts. Being found guilty in a trial by jury, Officer Henry pronounced a sentence of capital punishment, which was immediately carried out by hanging them from two oak trees on the courthouse lawn. The town watched silently. No one spoke aloud, but many heads nodded in agreement when the executions were carried out. Justice had been done.

Word of the 877th horrific ordeal was carried by messenger to Sergeant Major Roland in Jacksonport. He was willing to support the 877th stationed in Oak Ridge against any DHS aggression if he was able. Although he was still undermanned dealing with riots in the city, he sent the militia messenger back with two packages showing his support. SSG Mosby lifted the olive drab cases, almost 40 pounds each, without realizing what they were at first. Then he noticed. Stenciled in black lettering on the side, the model and nomenclature: FIM 92 Infrared Homing SAM. The 877th now had two Stinger missiles in its inventory.

The envoy sent to Jacksonville Air Force Base had returned. The militia envoy had gained entrance on the base, and showed the video testimony to the Air National Guard commander. Appalled by what he had seen, the commander spoke in confidence to the militiaman. The Air National Guard at Jacksonville was walking a tight rope of command. Three Colonels had already disappeared from the base. Asking questions about their disappearance could secure a person that same fate. Although he fell under the President's authority, he nonetheless did not approve of the federal government's actions. There were others in the active Air force that felt the same, but they needed to be careful. Radio frequencies were traded. A code word was established if the Air Guard had been compromised. That was as much as the Air Guard commander could do. For now.

Mixed word had come from the south. Pleasant Valley still had a city government and police department operational. Before the Meltdown, that government and police department had consisted of a mayor, treasurer, secretary and 4 part time officers. Now 25 part-time officers did what they could working with local towns people to fend off marauders from nearby Waynemont. The owners of House Manufacturing, located in this small town of 700, were eager to say they would support farmer operation with any needed equipment. And that town happened to have an operational locomotive engine with seven empty boxcars. The bad news was that Waynemont had literally gone to hell. The federal government had activated the Guard unit, eliminated it, and taken all equipment. The National Guard Armory in Waynemont was abandoned and there was no law and order in the town. Entire communities had been looted and burned. People were murdered for what little they had. There was a rumor that a local gang was controlling the south side of the city.

Finally, a citizen group from Oak Ridge had approached Highfield Seed Company for possible support. The owner was more than willing to help, but an agent from the nearby "Department of Agriculture Research Facility," who had shown up uninvited, was adamant that any help would be considered treasonous. The owner made a simple observation to the agent: "If you arrest the people growing the food, how will anyone be able to eat." The agent was upset, befuddled by the simplicity of the man, and left the seed company talking to himself. No one else, it seemed, was listening. Similar support came from about a dozen farmers. With no direction, they needed a reason to plant. Oak Ridge and the Northside Store provided them with direction and a market for their crops. Trade with neighboring towns such as Pleasant Valley and its farm implement company sweetened the deal.

* * *

The Declaration

New Year's Day saw Jason making his way to Oak Ridge for a town meeting. The morning was cold, testifying that December was only a taste of the bitter weather yet to come. A town meeting was held at the Oak Ridge Church of Christ auditorium, where over 100 citizens were in attendance. The business of this meeting was quite simple: to declare to their fellow Arkansans and everyone else why they had chosen to actively and aggressively resist the federal government. This course of action was, needless to say, risky business, but Oak Ridge was already at risk. By defending itself against attack by government forces, the town had taken a stand, refusing to submit to oppression. Now Oak Ridge needed others to stand by her side. Although present, the mayor was remarkably silent, sitting in the back row during the course of the meeting.

Representatives from nearby towns were also in attendance to witness the meeting, including Colonel Fernandez, and a Mr. James House, CEO of Pleasant Valley's House Manufacturing. Also unofficially present were two senior enlisted Air guardsmen from Jacksonville Air Force Base, personally vouched for by the Air Guard Commander. The Command Sergeant Major from the 39th Infantry Brigade Combat Team out of Camp Robinson made his way to Jason before the meeting, explaining that he was sympathetic and grateful for the rescue of the 877th. Jason looked the sergeant major in the eye. "They are your men, Sergeant Major. Why doesn't your general stand up for them?"

The sergeant major looked back at Jason, pausing. "He did. He and all his staff have been missing for two months. My men and I are in hiding, fighting back wherever we can." The CSM managed a smile. "I thought maybe I might get a lesson from you, Master Sergeant." Jason shook his hand and smiled. "Welcome to the resistance, Sergeant Major."

During the course of the meeting, a petition was presented. It stated:

As our Nation's founding fathers have eloquently noted, the purpose of any government is to secure the people's rights of life, liberty, and their pursuit of happiness. We, the people of Oak Ridge, hold our country in high esteem, recognizing that it has continually secured these rights. To the United States we rightly and gladly pledge our allegiance. Nevertheless, in the last three months, there are those in our federal government who have violated the very rights they have sworn to uphold and protect. These federal governing bodies have tolerated, instigated, and directed acts of murder, rape, and neglect against its own people: Specifically:

1. The federal government's Department of Homeland Security has usurped local authorities, torturing and murdering those who voice opposition.
2. That same Department of Homeland Security has withheld basic needs of both food and shelter from the citizens of Middleton as a means to obtain unconstitutional advantage and control over them.
3. That same Department had tortured and executed members of our State's National Guardsmen and local law enforcement agencies for not complying with their grievous tactics mentioned above.
4. Federal forces have employed the use of third parties to maintain control through the use of thuggery, brute force, and criminal conduct.
5. Warrantless searches have been conducted en masse by the federal government, which have been used to both punish citizens and deprive them of their sustenance and means of defense.
6. Rights of the accused have been routinely violated as a matter of course with our citizens not represented at a trial, without any recourse for justice, and subject to summary execution.
7. The Department of Homeland Security has launched military style attacks against the good and peaceful people of this town, both killing and injuring our citizens.

Numerous and sundry accounts of the above mentioned federal actions, which violate both our citizens' enumerated constitutional rights and those of human dignity, are witnessed to and supported with ample evidence in bound documentation underneath this declaration. Because of these atrocities committed, it is our view that

> such a tyrannical government does not represent the welfare of its people and therefore does not represent these United States. Against such tyranny, we hereby make our stand, pledging our allegiance to the true United States of America with our very lives if necessary.

The declaration was intentionally direct, stating facts. When the last sentence of the declaration was read, however, there was some murmuring in the auditorium. A rather plump, balding man seated near the back, questioned its wording:

"I mean really, the words 'our very lives.' Is that part necessary?"

SSG Moses, still gaunt and weak from his captivity, had always been a man of few words, rose to speak. When he rose, the room quieted. In a deep, powerful, voice that betrayed a heavy local accent, he simply declared: "Yes, it *is* necessary." Everyone in the room knew he spoke for many that could not speak for themselves. His words ended all debate. When the meeting was over, eighty-four people had signed the document. Clearly legible at the top of the list were the names of Jason Hamilton, Kenneth Mosby, Brian Henry, and Jeb Walker.

As they left the room that day, SSG Mosby joked with Jason about the declaration. "Should have known. Leave it to a school teacher to come up with something that sounds like it was taken from a history textbook." Jason laughed back but they both knew, everyone knew, the serious nature of what they had just done.

* * *

The Guard Center Raid

During the month of December, Officer Henry, now the Oak Ridge Chief of Police, had been busy. Where he was responsible for law-enforcement within the town, Henry also understood the prisoners he housed had valuable, time-sensitive information. Although he did not resort to torture tactics during interrogations, Henry employed much more sinister tactics: the smell of steaks cooking outside the jail and the promise of a hot shower proved to loosen quite a few tongues. The resulting information had been a veritable treasure trove of information regarding DHS's supply, routines, and goals. Part of that information had been about the 32 men working at the Guard armory. They had been coerced to work there through threats to their families. Corroborating information from other prisoners confirmed what had been said. In short, the refugees' husbands had been found.

When Officer Henry informed Jason about this, Jason knew something must be done. He and others at Bo Hill had celebrated Christmas with the broken families. Although, the women and children had been thankful, there was still an unspoken question: Would their families ever be whole again? That question had haunted Jason throughout the holidays as he was recovering from his wound. Now, although he was still somewhat limited in his mobility, Jason knew he had to act.

Bo Hill would lead the rescue mission. Oak Ridge would also support the mission with equipment, including night vision, and fuel, which was becoming more and more scarce. The primary goal of the mission was to rescue the mechanics. If possible, a secondary goal would be to disable or destroy equipment, impeding DHS mission performance. There would be two parties in this plan. An initial recon and infiltration group would attempt to contact the hostage workers. The recon group would inform the main raid party as to enemy positions, strength, and disposition of workers. Although Jason wanted to spearhead the recon group, SSG Mosby kicked Jason's cane to make a point. So Jason would be with the main raiding party. "Don't worry, Mr. Jason. I do a good job for you," Juan said, smiling. And so began this second rescue mission.

It was a cold January afternoon. Juan grimaced from the wind biting his face. The sun would set soon. Juan had already identified the hostage mechanics earlier that day, working on the tracked vehicles. He had been able to make contact with one of the workers that morning who was performing a wintertime preventive maintenance service. Juan gave him three letters, handwritten by the refugees and addressed to their husbands.

The man left and another came back. "Is it true that Amanda and the kids are free?" the second man asked. Juan nodded. "They stay down the street from me and my family. I have 32 names. We come to free the people on this list." Juan showed the man.

"Yes, they are all here. We work from 6:00 a.m. until 9:00 p.m. every day. There are guards with radios around the edge of the facility. We were told if we attempted escape, they would kill our wives or children."

"You must wait. When it time, we need your help."

Twenty-six NSA and 32 prisoners were running the maintenance facility. The National Guard Armory, now known at the "NSA Maintenance Center," was responsible for maintaining all federal government vehicles in Middleton. Skilled federal workers had been stretched thin so the "creative" use of hostage workers was considered "thinking outside the box." Today, however, the mechanics themselves had been thinking outside the box, spending the entire day covertly sabotaging equipment. That day would prove to be a long, tiring day of "maintenance."

The raid itself was a serious risk. Sixteen of the twenty-six guards worked the outside of the perimeter in four guard towers. They looked similar to the tower at the county jail, being manned by two guards each. The towers appeared to be equipped with .50 caliber machine guns. Jason assumed each tower would have scope-mounted night vision, as well. The bottom line was that the towers must be taken out immediately, if there were to be any hope of mission success. There were also eight men that patrolled the perimeter of the maintenance facility, two men patrolling each side of the facility's main building parking lots. The patrols were armed with M4s and what the prisoners termed machine guns, most likely the M256 Squad Automatic Weapon. The ten remaining guards were inside, rotating shifts with the tower and patrols as well as acting as a quick reaction force. In the drill hall of the reserve center, there were 150 NSA agents who could act as a near immediate relief force during the evening, if necessary.

It was the early hours of the morning when the 9-man rescue team penetrated the chain link of the motor pool's west perimeter fence. Moving through the parking lot, they silently took up positions to eliminate the two-man roving patrols. At exactly 3:00 a.m., Jason gave the signal over the radio. 4 AT-4s were launched at the guard towers. Three towers exploded immediately. One missile launcher, however, had misfired. Luckily the remaining tower was in range of Jason's hummer. William trained the heavy .50 caliber gun upon the guard post, opening fire with ½ inch diameter armor-piercing projectiles. The machine gun, designed to penetrate armor, easily destroyed the sandbagged wooden tower, which actually split down the middle before it fell to the ground. Moving his vehicle forward, Jason drove to the front of the drill hall while the other hummer covered the rear. Although the two hummers could not effectively contain the 150 agents within the center, Jason and Juan's vehicle-mounted guns began to wreak havoc on the DHS personnel as they began to run out of the back doors of the facility, trying to assist their comrades in the maintenance bay.

The eight-man team, using night vision, had managed to target half of the roving guards. The remaining guards on the east side of the maintenance bay, however, were joined by most of the quick reaction force within the building. Although under heavy fire from Bo Hill's hummer-mounted SAWs and M60s, the besieged guards had found refuge behind the M113 tracked troop transports. Jason saw the M113s and hated to leave them behind, but he knew there was no way to escape and evade with a 27,000 pound tracked vehicle.

In spite of the way William and Philip had been steadily pouring fire into the reserve center entrances, more agents were making it outside. Jason felt he had woken up a hornet's nest. They had stuck a good blow, but if the rescue party did not leave soon, it would be annihilated.

Inside the maintenance bay, the workers had been freed by four of the 8-man team. A firefight broke out between the rescue team and two DHS agents who had remained inside. Two of the team went down from assault rifle fire before the DHS threat was neutralized. One of the rescued workers, however, ran back toward the opposite entrance, away from the fighting. About 90 seconds later, the sound of a heavy diesel engine was heard above the gunfire. From the north side of the complex, though assaulted with all sorts of enemy small arms fire, a tracked vehicle rounded the corner of the maintenance bay. Inside, one heroic mechanic floored the throttle, plowing directly into the 14 remaining guards, running three of them over. At the same time, the maintenance doors opened up, and the 8-man rescue team engaged the remaining guards. Caught in the heavy crossfire, the DHS guards were mowed down. The M113 proceeded to the chain link gate, simply running it over. Four armored hummers rolled in behind the tracked vehicle, and to the giant overhead doors.

How many people can fit inside a hummer? That day 13 people could, with one gunner topside per vehicle. Although extra weapons had been brought, it was so cramped inside the vehicles that few could readily access them had they wanted. The hummers rolled up past the guard armory, exchanging fire with DHS agents of the relief force who, although pinned down by .50 caliber fire, were returning fire from the cover of the next building. When Juan and Philip's vehicle stopped engaging the Reserve Center and pulled away, security agents rushed en mass for the maintenance facility. Vehicles were fired up, and made their way out the smashed gate in pursuit. Jason waived the others to the east. The plan was simple. Hit and run. Disburse. Make cover ASAP at separate predetermined locations to avoid air recon. Move at evening. Evade and make it to Oak Ridge.

Jason's vehicle remained behind, with William raining the last of the .50 caliber rounds down on the pursuit convoy, which was exiting via the smashed gate. Out of ammo, William jumped down into the hummer and came back up with an M256. He began firing it, resting it on the armored roof of the hummer's cab, while Jason moved forward at a steady 40 miles per hour in an attempt to buy the rescued workers time. After a moment, Jason pulled on William's leg to signal time to roll. Jason's hummer sped up, with the enemy convoy in unhindered pursuit.

What had happened the previous day had, until then, gone unnoticed. That Tuesday had been a particularly heavy maintenance day for the maintenance workers. The entire morning had been spent changing oil and fluids on the M113s. In actuality, every hose of the tracked vehicles had been cut, every fitting broken. The entire M113 line had been sabotaged, rendered inoperative. The workers had sabotaged the hummers and lighter vehicles some other way. Somehow the mechanics had clogged the exhaust. In less than two minutes, the hummers began to sputter, and burst into flames. Never underestimate the ingenuity of motivated mechanics.

After about a mile, the engines of every pursuit vehicle had stalled. The hundred or so DHS agents who had been in pursuit, were without a ride. They began to walk back to the reserve center, some only in their underwear. The raid had been a success, with all rescue vehicles away from immediate harm. But in their return home, Jason could not help thinking about the M113s.

The M113s had long been replaced for infantry support by the M2 and M3 Bradley Fighting Vehicle, which possessed greater speed, armor, and firepower. Since the Iraq and Afghanistan wars, however, the Army had seen fit to centralize much of their wartime equipment. Most Bradleys were at Fort Hood, Texas. This left many of the M113s, which still played an active role in with combat engineers and other combat support, at local units. Apparently, DHS had been collecting these older armored vehicles in Middleton. Jason wondered what would happen if Oak Ridge's defenses had to stand up against armor. In fact, although Jason did not know it, Oak Ridge had less than two months before they were to find out.

The welcome home had been a mixed affair. Five families mourned the loss of their loved ones, including the Gilberts, who lived down Pine View near the Everlings. Still there was an air of celebration. Families who had been unjustly separated had been reunited. For most, it was a late New Year's present. For Jason, it was his birthday.

8 THE HUNGRY HORDE

Food was now the chief concern of everyone. Oak Ridge, Bo Hill, and other outlying districts were strictly rationing their provisions. For Bo Hill, who had taken in 124 people, this was of pressing concern. The price of food shot up when bought at the Oak Ridge market. There was simply little supply. Local farmers, most on the west side of the ridge were helping out, but there was also a fuel shortage. The silos at the Everling Farm were half empty, and now Bo Hill had been blessed with 40 more mouths to feed. The sheep and goats now had 7 new additions, and every time Jason looked at them he saw lamb chops. Still, the herd needed to increase. If they gave away everything now, they would have nothing later. Fishing was no longer a local pastime. A 30-acre lake on the edge of Deer Run Road was a popular spot, even in the bitter cold of January. Fishing was such a necessity that 6 fishhooks could be traded for a blanket.

It happened at the end of January. Robert called Jason on the radio. Apparently, a large crowd was walking from the city of Tuckerville through the fields, coming their way. Robert, who lived about 2 miles from the ridge on Pine View Road, had seen them coming. The muster for Bo Hill was sounded. Jason drove out with 15 others in two hummer, armed to the teeth. Whatever was happening, Robert's rice bins must be protected. If not, everyone at Bo Hill would starve. One vehicle and twelve of the men remained at the farm. Robert jumped in Jason's hummer. The crowd was about a half a mile away. As the hummer grew closer, Jason noticed they were carrying shovels, hammers, hoes, machetes, and anything else that could be wielded as a weapon. It was a desperate crowd of misery.

Pulling near the crowd of about 100 people, Jason mounted the gunner's seat, with a 5.56 Squad Automatic Weapon mounted on turret. "This land is under the protection of Bo Hill. State your business."

"We are starving. That is our business. Give us food," the leader of the rough and ragged group yelled back angrily. The man, thin as he was, appeared strong and resolute. Ironically, the man was wearing a Motley Crue t-shirt. Jason then looked to the crowd and beyond. Small groups of men were traveling behind them over the frozen fields. There must be 300 men that Jason could see. It was obvious what had caused this exodus. Starvation. The system they had been relying on to feed them and keep them warm had failed. There was simply no possibility of feeding the mass that followed and still survive the winter. But there was something else unusual about the crowd. There were no women, no children. Something was wrong.

"We would like to help. If you send representatives to talk with us, we can talk about assistance..."

A gunshot sounded from the Macannally place about 200 yards away, then Jason could see two people running. Mrs. Macanally, whose husband had died liberating those at the Middleton armory, was running from their mobile home. Her teenage daughter, with a shotgun in hand, ran with her. About a dozen men began pouring through the front door of their trailer, then three machete-wielding men ran out the back door, in pursuit of the pair.

"We have talked enough. We will eat," the leader said, showing his yellowed teeth. Horror dawned upon Jason's face as he realized that the man was wearing a necklace strung with ears...human ears. The leader then gave a savage cry and a dozen men rushed the hummer.

"Gun it. Pick them up." Jason managed a quick burst from the hummer's automatic weapon as the hummer accelerated. One man had managed to jump on the hood of the vehicle. Jason pulled his 9mm and shot the man in the neck. Bright red blood sprayed across the hood of the hummer. The hummer spun frozen gravel on the angry mob and bounced over the frozen earth as it accelerated. A second man had managed to somehow wedge his hand in the rear passenger door handle and was being dragged along the field. Jason attempted to take aim with his sidearm, but it was unnecessary. The assailant's legs caught under the rear wheel of the hummer, resulting in a human speed bump that almost threw Jason from the gunner's well. The distance between the hummer and the two fleeing women shortened. Driving behinds the two women, the hummer literally ran upon the first of the pursuers. A rather corpulent redheaded man, in a summer dress and a white trash bag, had been singularly intent on catching a meal. The oddly dressed fellow hit the hummer's brush guard with a thud and was killed instantly. His body, however stuck there for a moment. As the vehicle slowed to a stop, Jason noticed the dead man's bloody maniacal grimace. The dead man reminded Jason of an insane clown he had once read about in a Stephen King novel. The hummer stopped for a moment, and both opposite passenger doors opened. The two remaining pursuers, taken back for a moment, looked at Jason, then their mass of comrades racing toward them behind the vehicle. It was as if they were deciding what they should do. The pair then looked to each other and resumed their maddened charge but were quickly dispatched by the combined efforts of Juan's M4 and Jason's 9mm Browning. As Mrs. Macanally and her teenage daughter jumped in the vehicle, and they raced back toward Everling farm,

Robert looked bewildered. "What is going on, Jason?" Jason's response brought horror to Robert's face. "They were going to eat them."

The hummer continued due west across the open field while, behind them, some of the mob had continued in pursuit. Others, Jason observed, appeared to be concerned for their fallen comrades' welfare. Then Jason saw one kneeling man raise a rather large ax. The crowd was not concerned. The crowd was hungry.

Driving in front of the Everling farm, Jason shouted instructions for some of the awaiting men to get on the roof of the house. Another climbed the rice silo. Parking the hummer by the front of their home, Jason radioed the Bo Hill and Oak Ridge, warning them of danger to their east. "Muster to treeline of the hills. Call muster for Highfield. These are evil men," Jason's voice sounded chilled over the static of the radio. "Cannibals."

And so began a four-hour siege of the Everling farm. Jason and Robert simply had no choice. The rice stores were the lifeblood of Bo Hill. There was no reasoning with this hunger-maddened crowd. At first, one or two people would try to run toward Robert's home and barn, an ax or a stick in hand. Robert, aiming his own 30.06 out the hummer's window, shouted, pleaded with the hunger-crazed lunatics to leave. The mob seemed to have lost all reason and any humanity as well. When the mob would move into the Everling's yard, the men on the roof would drop them immediately. More would take their place. From the front window, Sue witnessed the event. Robert saw her crying in the living room, and went in to comfort his wife. They both cried together.

More knots of people made their way around the farm, trying to attack it from the west, by the grain bins, but it was a hopeless massacre. The hunger-crazed people stood no chance. Apparently the group had no firearms. After a while, the groups of people realized they were simply wasting both their energy and their lives and tried to bypass the farm. Jason realized that if those men were allowed to cross to the hills, Bo Hill and Oak Ridge would be subject to constant threat. Bo Hill was radioed again. All men in the eastern defensive muster were to form a skirmish line and move out east. Any human contact was to be brought down. Period.

From a bird's eye, the view was as follows: The 54 men and teenage boys of Bo Hill, along with 50 men from Highfield walked together at 50 foot intervals for the better part of a mile, converging on any resistance, and conducting "mop up" operations. Further to the east, across the #10 drainage ditch, the two hummers chased down knots of the hunger-driven savages. It was a slaughter, necessary, and without any hint of glory. Any of those men who survived the two hummers were systematically hunted down that day. Some of the hunger-crazed men tried to attack, and were shot down like the animals they were. Some tried to surrender. They too were gunned down.

That day, no mercy was shown. A line had been crossed regarding what must be done to survive, and crossing that line had been a necessity. The air was too cold to melt the frost that winter day, and the sun shone against the frozen grass, making the land sparkle like fields of diamonds. The only flaws to this winter wonderland were human bodies, red with blood, the occasional popcorn of small arms fire, and the smell of gunpowder, which hung heavy in the air, like the guilt in the hearts of the men of Bo Hill.

The day darkened, and night began as men continued their perimeter vigil. Jason wondered to himself if any man in Bo Hill would have been able to sleep anyway. The people on Pine View Road stayed at the Everling farm. From survivor reports, this group of hunger-crazed men had left headed west, murdering everyone in their path along the way. Stopping the madness of these men was a grim necessity to protect both their families and their food supply. Still, grown men cried that night standing watch, thinking about the slaughter. The teens in the group questioned their fathers why this had to be. Fathers answered their sons, "To survive."

* * *

February

February brought warmer weather to Bo Hill, and there was already talk of getting in an early potato crop. Jason had guarded his potato cache jealously, having the entire storm shelter covered with boxes of potatoes sprouting eye buds. Just a few more weeks perhaps, to ensure the frost doesn't get them. "Cover them with hay, and they will be protected and still stay warm," Juan advised. By the second week of February, the potatoes had already been cut and placed into the ground. Juan warned not to plant them too deep in the tilled soil, but simply cover them with hay." "That way there is not weeds, Mr. Jason. The ground stays wet."

The issue of overcrowding was a big concern at the town meeting. Bo Hill had grown from 27 people to 168 people over the winter. There was no skirting around the issue. The houses on Ricker Road, which had originally held 12 people each, were now housing about eighteen people each. Conditions were unsanitary, and the flu season was still upon them. Seven women and children were seriously ill as a result. A subsistence diet of rice had not helped the matter. In addition, with so many people forced to live under one roof, there had been "personality conflicts." A few more notable personalities were "traded off" to other houses simply because they could not be tolerated. One of the factors that had originally necessitated the cramped conditions was heating. There were simply not enough stoves. Another factor which called for such cramped quarters was security: the ability to defend each home.

Now, with the promise of warmer weather and most families back together, there was a need for more room. Ten remaining houses on Deer Run Road still stood vacant. Hesitantly, Robert pointed out that there were four houses on Pine View east of the Macanally residence that had become unoccupied. The fate of those residents had not been mentioned, but all somberly remembered the events of last week. Some houses were solid and well maintained. Some not so well. What was fair? Jason thought about the issue, having become the de facto "mayor" of sorts after Officer Henry had moved to Oak Ridge.

Twenty houses for forty families. How could they solve this problem? First it was asked if anyone wanted to leave Bo Hill. Jason pointed out that staying in Bo Hill meant obligations to both provide for one's own family and for the security of the group. Secondly, Jason noted, since Bo Hill was in active rebellion against federal authorities, simply living here could be considered treason. Finally Jason spoke of property rights. Everyone at Bo Hill except for two families only had squatter's rights to where they currently lived. Although, no family would be tossed out in the cold, the rightful owners could perhaps return to contest their property later on. After Jason's most eloquent persuasion, no one volunteered to leave.

Jason then brought forth a second proposal after much discussion among the refugees. He proposed that Bo Hill be "officially" recognized as its own township, and that a committee be formed to address township boundaries and also solve the housing crisis. After two days, the committee had reached their decisions. Bo Hill was officially recognized. It was to encompass:

> All land between Big Creek and Church Creek up to Pine View Road east. More specifically it included two squares of 680 acres, one on each side of the highway. In the northeast, Bo Hill would include a thirteen acre pond and a 4 acre pond on the west side surrounded by about 90 acres of woods. Smaller ponds and wooded areas were throughout. South of there lay about 240 acres of pasture land with mixed woods. On the east, Bo Hill would contain about 560 acres of farmland and about 50 acres of wooded area.

All of these lands would not be homesteaded, and would be considered in trust of the community. Those lands could potentially be leased or bought outright only by individuals within the community. Hunting, trapping, fishing, and limited logging for fuel outside the homesteaded lands were considered community rights.

Homestead Properties: All homesteaded properties were to

include approximately seven acres so home gardens could be grown and properly developed. Property would not be gerrymandered but would observe existing boundaries whenever possible.

    The committee determined the only fair way to settle the housing problem was a lottery drawing. Since no families wanted to leave, two families would coexist within one homestead. This meant partnerships. Families were asked to find people they could get along with. A week went by. People discussed advantages, skills, and work ethics. It was to their advantage to choose wisely. Others who could not find partner families were paired up. Volunteer partnerships were asked for homesteading Pine View Road. It was good flat ground for growing but was relatively defenseless. Also, wood for fuel was lacking. Two volunteers agreed to homestead on Pine View under the condition that they could homestead 14 acres each. That meant two more homesteads of the same size would be needed when the lottery was drawn. Robert winced but agreed, since it meant giving up 28 acres of his own land. It also, however, meant neighbors who might work for him and provide security. After all, he did own 2000 acres of farmland.

    The lottery was kept public, held right in Jason's front yard at noon the next Sunday. Some drew beautiful houses; others received mobile homes, all of them needed supplies. Two large outbuildings at Bo Hill had been turned into warehouses of sorts, maintained by both Juan and William. It was agreed that the goods, which had been signed for by the original housekeepers, would be divided up equally among the partnerships of each house. Blankets, canned goods, and various goods that had been taken from each of the houses beforehand were equally distributed. Juan and William earned their degrees in record keeping, accounting for the accuracy of each item. Although, the items were now the property of the partnerships, inevitable disputes of fairness would arise, so the records were open to the public.

    Jason was well aware of the problems associated with blind charity. The refugees were now a part of Bo Hill, but each partnership would need to work the land and provide for their own. Robert originally had agreed to donate crop seed for the first year's corn crop with the promise of a return. Jason intended to keep that agreement. Robert would receive 1/3 of the harvest for that year and help from each partnership with processing the corn into meal. That would be about 10,000 bushels of corn, a portion of which would be used for seed corn, but a larger portion would be used to trade with Oak Ridge, Waltersville, and Pleasant Valley, with the Everling Farm keeping the proceeds. 55,000 pounds of cornmeal would purchase a lot in this economy.

Tuesday Meltdown

Jason had made it home that evening to his wife. It seemed that the month of February had been flying by. He was thankful to be alive. He was thankful for his family being safe. William had mostly recovered from his wound, although taking more time than Jason. William still had pain in his left collarbone, and only time would mend the broken bone. Most of all, however, Jason was thankful for his wife.

There had been some quiet times after he and William had returned injured. When Jason had initially told Deborah of his plan to free the prisoners at the armory, the two had fought. Deborah had yelled, "I have to lose my husband so these women we barely even know can have theirs!" Then quiet for two days before she spoke again. One evening, Deborah had come to bed early and simply said with a flirty voice, "Well, if you are going to kill yourself saving the world, you better get a nice going away present." Jason had left the next day. That had been over a month ago. Today, however, was a day to be remembered.

For days, Jason had been searching for something extremely rare in this new economy. He had shot a beaver and walked overland 4 ½ miles to Oak Ridge under the pretense of conferencing with SSG Mosby. He resisted the temptation to simply take the meat and go home. It would have been a welcome change. Instead, he arrived at the Northside Market with the field-dressed game. He held up his beaver at the front counter: "I want to buy a giant cookie. Do you have chocolate chips?"

As Jason was making his way home, his wound had opened up a bit, and a deep biting pain set in. He was mumbling something about the fuel shortage when he began hobbling up his driveway. By the time he reached the front door, however, his composure changed. Opening the door, he called out, "Baby, I love you. Happy Valentine's Day." Deborah of course knew what day it was. She had simply thought he had forgotten. Tears were in her beautiful blue eyes. "Honey, I love you so much." They held each other in the dining room, looking at the sunset through the window. "Baby, I am going to get you that bay window you always wanted, too. I haven't forgotten." Deborah laughed at the silly thought. That had been the topic of conversation immediately before the Tuesday Meltdown had occurred. Then she noticed his bloody leg. "Baby," Jason said. "Do you still have some of those Ibuprofen?"

"You are crazy, man," Deborah was beaming. "Crazy, I tell ya."

Jason was on the couch with his leg propped up. The medication had finally kicked in, and he was enjoying a pain-free rest.

"Umm, Dad?" It was Peter. Jason's youngest son had not been acting all together right for the last two months. Considering all the events Peter had been through, that was to be expected. Hell, everyone had been put through the wringer. The hunger-crazed mob two weeks ago had driven most everyone at Bo Hill to the edge of sanity, it seemed.

"Dad, I wanted to talk with you. Deborah already knows." Jason looked to his wife, and she nodded, smiling seriously. "Dad, I think I am in love." Jason was relieved it was not something worse. "Well, tell me about her, son."

"You know that girl, Jessica Macannally."

"Umm, yeah. She and her mom stay at William's."

"Well, umm, I hunt squirrels."

Jason wondered what squirrels had to do with this girl. He listened as his son told the story of how he had met her one day at the edge of a ditch. She had been fishing. He had been hunting. Long story short, Peter had been giving this girl squirrels for almost two months now.

"And she loves me, too."

Who could argue against the young couple? His son had won the heart of a woman with dead rodents. Sounded about right for this crazy, new world. As Jason listened, Deborah held his hand. His son spoke of how he had met Jessica. Jason watched Peter's eyes light up every time he spoke her name. At that moment, Jason realized that, in spite of no running water nor electricity, without knowing if his family would survive through tomorrow, he could not possibly be happier than he was at that moment.

* * *

The Broadcast

Liberated AM and FM radio stations had announced the program for weeks in advance. Now Jason's family listened quietly to Ben Decker's final broadcast. The shortwave radio cackled static as the radio broadcaster spoke. Mr. Decker had chosen to broadcast even though he knew DHS forces were close and tracking him "...because it is not the role of government to patronize nor terrorize its citizens. It is rather the citizens, empowered with their God-given rights, among which are life, liberty, and the pursuit of happiness, who should direct their own lives, empowering the government as *they* see fit."

"But no, this current administration has come against any one who dares breathe the dangerous words of liberty. They have come after me. My home has been bombed. My oldest son was murdered while in jail. And, I... I am simply a lone voice calling out somewhere in the wilderness... This totalitarian regime tramples the rights of the people of this land, murdering opposition and looting for its own self-preservation. And such a regime has the audacity to call itself the United States of America? A government of the people, by the people, and for the people? Ladies and gentlemen, this government is not *our* America. And now I call upon you to take a stand, the same stand I take this day, and take *our* America back."

Mr. Decker spoke of world news. How China had gone no further in its aggression against the United States, Japan, and Taiwan. It had its own troubles. Rice imports from the United States had simply vanished. 1.3 billion Chinese, accustomed to a more affluent life, were now lined up around buildings to receive rationed food. Food riots in China had been quelled by tanks, yet tanks could not be everywhere. Chinese oil imports from the Middle East were being plagued by piracy off the coasts of Ethiopia, Sudan, and elsewhere in the Indian Ocean. There were unconfirmed rumors that this piracy had been a covert effort of India.

Closer to home, Mr. Decker reported a United States in conflict. In California and Washington state, things were somewhat stable. The federal government had instituted marshal law in California, and fired upon looters rioting in East L. A., killing over 400 people. Owning a gun or hoarding food was a capital offense. People were expected to line up and behave, and on the west coast, for the most part, they did so. Washington D.C. had experienced rioting in the streets when the SNAP program had failed early on. Yet the facade of a caring government slipped away as the president had ordered Marines to fire upon D.C. residents. There had been few problems in the capital city after that show of force. In fact, there were no reports at all until New Year, since the national media, who were at one time in the pocket of the president, were now under his thumb. Local governments in cities such as New York, Philadelphia, and Baltimore were falling right in line to receive what little federal welfare they could, which was very little.

Decker explained that the president had been hesitant about calling upon the military for assistance. On many Army bases, small wars had erupted when the military was ordered to suppress U.S. citizens. Fort Leonard Wood, Missouri had totally rejected federal authority and there had been a failed attempt to assassinate the post's commanding general. In response, the general had these words: "If you want this post, you will have to nuke it." In Fort Campbell, Kentucky the president had called upon the 5th Army Special Forces Group to quell a rebellion in Nashville. Senior noncoms defied those orders, remembering their motto: "To Liberate the Oppressed." The convoy bound for Nashville simply stopped in its tracks, and any officer voicing opposition was shot. The convoy turned back around and a bloody conflict ensued, with no clear winner. This resulted in DHS forces fleeing Nashville, being unable to control the city on their own.

The Department of Homeland Security was not without its own victories, however, Decker explained. In the suburbs of Chicago, Illinois guardsmen and militia tried to blockade Interstate 55. DHS helicopter gunships and Bradley fighting vehicles had decimated the resistance. Some opposition forces were being summarily executed for treason. Others were sent to federal detainment centers. When Jason heard this, he winced. He had seen such facilities first hand.

Everyone in the living room listened to the radio, knowing how this particular broadcast would end. "....However, we are not without hope, America. In places such as the Midwest and the southern United States, federal government forces are losing their foothold. State governments in Texas, Oklahoma, Louisiana, Mississippi, and Alabama have simply refused to recognize this totalitarian regime. To the citizens of those states, I salute you. Iowa and Missouri are organizing resistance, as well. I call upon the citizens of those states and others to stand for justice. And ladies and gentlemen, in the state of Arkansas, there is a little town named Oakland, no wait, it's Oak Ridge...Oak Ridge, Arkansas. There, an American Flag flies along with a red ribbon. That ribbon is said to represent Americans who have fought and died for freedom. And in that same town, the citizens speak of a man, no a hero, who fights oppression and sets prisoners free... God bless you, sir."

Jason sat back in the corner of his living room, blushing. "Dad," Philip whispered. "He is talking about you." Jason said nothing.

"I do not have much time left," Ben Decker continued. "DHS vehicles have just pulled up my driveway. I do not expect to live. But, I am offering no resistance. I am leaving the resistance to you, the people of these United States of America. Goodbye and..." The broadcast continued with some shouting in the background. Gunfire, sounding like popping over the radio. A loud shout, then louder popping followed by the white noise of static.

* * *

9 SABOTAGE AT RICELAND RAILHEAD

The cold of the late February night had chilled Jason as he and SSG Mosby were observing the Riceland facility. What was even more chilling, however, were the several flatbed railroad cars at the Riceland railroad complex, or perhaps better said, the content of those cars: three Apache gunships and two Bradley fighting vehicles. Jason recalled worrying about DHS possibly using Blackhawk helicopters and M113s. Comparing M113s to Bradleys was like comparing crossbows to assault rifles. What chance had Oak Ridge, Jacksonport, or anyone else against these new weapons? These weapons needed to be destroyed, or everything was lost. Remaining in place, Jason and SSG Mosby radioed Oak Ridge. More men and equipment were needed. And plastic explosives.

The two teams had arrived the next night, but there was no possibility of having all 18 men penetrate the southern perimeter. The relocation of the Middleton's downtown district residents had occurred two months ago. It had been Homeland Security's ironic way of celebrating Christmas, the forcing of 150 families out of their homes. The reason: to increase security around the Riceland railroad complex after the recent attack on the nearby jail. And the relocation had indeed increased security. Roving patrols had planned their routes through the old neighborhood, leaving no street unobserved. Coming within five blocks of the railroad complex appeared impossible.

"Master Sergeant, how are we going to make it there. They are watching all the streets," Private Davenport had whispered while they were kneeling behind a row of hedges.

"We go under the streets." Jason pointed to a manhole cover. It took almost 90 minutes for the six men to crawl the five blocks of sewer system, which, by comparison, was not a very long time. Recon militia had spent days at a time mapping the underground passageways, meticulously recording their navigated routes on plastic sheets with permanent marker.

The truth was, a Sharpie and a crayon were about the only technology that could function in that wet, filthy environment. Three conduits had been discovered which would allow good visibility of the rail complex. Jason had taken the shortest route.

Now Jason, Juan, and Private Davenport, along with three other volunteers were eying the 5 flatbed railroad cars with a clear line of sight. If the railroad cars only had contained choppers, AT4 rocket launchers would have worked well for sabotage. The Bradleys, however, would take most launched rockets like spitballs. Plastic explosives had to be positioned inside the engine compartment or the vehicle itself to significantly damage the Bradleys. That meant this sabotage operation had to be silent, up close, and personal. Two weapons fit the bill for that type of work: crossbows and knives.

The plan was simple enough. Small arms fire from the north of the facility would draw attention to the other side of the complex. With luck, some attention would be taken from the staged helicopters and fighting vehicles. The six-man team would eliminate the guards around the equipment and then blow the equipment in place. AT4s would destroy the choppers; C4 would disable the fighting vehicles.

As they had finished assembling the three crossbows, however, something had changed. The three guards patrolling the new equipment were met by three more guards. Now they had paired off in patrols of two. The 14-man assault force radioed in that two M113 with mounted .50 calibers had begun patrol at the front gate about fifteen minutes ago. Somehow DHS knew they were coming and had heightened their alert status. Just their luck, three crossbows and six guards. But the time to attack appeared to be now or never. Timing the guards to where only one patrol was visible, Jason signaled the attack just as Juan and Davenport fired.

Gunfire from across the vast complex marked the beginning. Jason and his men had to cross 50 yards across train tracks to reach the railroad cars. The two dead guards lay up ahead where he and three other militia were running to take cover. Four more guards were on the other side. One patrol appeared to be double timing around the train. Had they heard something? Jason reached the train just as one DHS patrol rounded the corner. Lying prone, Jason fired his crossbow...and missed. The two-man patrol saw him, raised their rifles, and suddenly and silently dropped down. Juan and Davenport were across the tracks. Jason tipped his hat. Juan returned his gesture by furiously waiving with both hands to "Go, go, go!"

Jason crouched to reload another crossbow bolt. Maybe he should have given this thing to someone else. Jason and two of the other militia climbed the railcars. The one remaining militia readied his assault rifle. Now it was Jason's time to waive furiously: "No, wait," he gestured with

Tuesday Meltdown

his free hand. The patrol on the other side were close to the railcars, but their attention was on the fire fight almost a quarter mile away.

"Why do they get all the fun?" one guard laughed.

"I would rather be at home than in some damn..." the unsuspecting guard was suddenly brought down by a militiaman jumping from the railcar. Hearing the commotion of his colleague's head being slammed into the gravel, the other turned to see what was wrong. Jason put a cross bolt through the man's chest. "Breathe, relax, squeeze." Jason thought. "I got this."

Bolt cutters? Jason reached into the Alice pack. Yes. 200 series locks? No problem. Jason worked his way over the tops of the Bradleys, cutting the driver hatchs' and engine hatchs' locks.

On the north side of the complex, SSG Mosby's men felt like they had attacked a bear with a broomstick. No sooner than they had started their sniping from the nearby concrete factory and electric station, did all hell break loose. Machine guns returned fire, as M113s moved directly across the railroad tracks to assault the aggressors. The assignment was simple, keep DHS forces busy for Jason and Juan. It had quickly turned into an affair of survival. They had no weaponry with them to take on even the light armor of the tracked vehicles. .50 caliber rounds slammed into the concrete culverts, turning them into rubble. The tracked vehicles seemed to be more careful around the electric station, however, and held their fire. The order to fall back was given, as enemy hummers moved in behind support of the APCs. The bait had been taken. Now the two assault teams had no choice but to retreat and evade capture. Falling into the hands of DHS would not be a pleasant experience.

Jason and the three militia had moved back beyond the tracks. C4 with det cord had been set to a single time fuse. They had approximately one minute left. Five of the six men disappeared down the manhole. Jason waited and watched. There were about 20 agents running toward the railcar. Would the explosives detonate? Then, five simultaneous, metal crumpling explosions. Damn, Jason loved det cord. He closed the manhole cover on top of him.

It took three hours crawling through sewer before Jason's team had made enough distance to be safe. From there, they moved quicker, making it to the rally point, Southwest Middleton, by dawn. There, Jason learned that five of the SSG Mosby's assault team had been killed and four were injured. Of the four wounded, one would not make the trip back to Oak Ridge. Given extra doses of morphine, the soldier had slipped away in the predawn hours. But what had happened? Somehow DHS had known something. Who was the leak that had tipped off Jason's raid?

That was the discussion during the next day at the courthouse.

"When were you planning to coordinate with Southwest on the

Murphy Refinery raid?" Jason asked SSG Mosby quietly.

"It is set for this Saturday evening, if weather holds. We have advanced recon planned with Jeb and Colonel Fernandez."

The Murphy Refinery was more than a raid. It was a coordinated grab at fuel supplies that would help Oak Ridge and the surrounding farms. Thus far, Oak Ridge had no electricity but more importantly, the farmers had little fuel for cultivating and planting crops. Where there once had been hope that the sergeant major in Jacksonport would be able to secure the nearby coal power plant, now it seems that Jacksonport was having difficulty maintaining law and order. Oak Ridge needed fuel. That meant securing the Murphy refinery and moving tankers in from the west.

"Mosby, who knows about this mission?" The answer to that question had to be very few people. Indeed the 877th had been conducting all its recent missions this way—a strict need-to-know basis. The unit always mobilized at the last minute. No warning--but always prepared. OPSEC was the operative word in this unit.

"I believe only Lieutenant Ryan knows," Mosby responded.

Jason was amazed with Ryan. Lieutenant Ryan had been tortured, losing two fingers, yet he still was "Mission First." It was as if the torture had galvanized his loyalty to his men. Jason would bet his life the lieutenant was not the leak. If he were the only one that knew, the mission would not be compromised.

"Oh, and the mayor. He knows, too."

Jason thought. Hmm. "Okay, but we need to do this, too." Jason and Mosby continued their conversation well into the evening.

10 THE SECOND BATTLE OF OAK RIDGE

That Saturday night brought a full moon and a full muster of the 877th. By 2:15 a.m., equipment was drawn, vehicles had been readied, and the 877th was moving north on Highway 1. When the convoy reached Highfield, the convoy turned east on Highfield Road. It was a standard recon radio check and COMSEC issue. Private Andre' would issue frequencies, call signs, challenge/password and radio microphones. Then he would ride with the last vehicle. Jason radioed in to Colonel Fernandez and Jeb using a scrambled frequency.

"Whiskey three niner this is juliet alpha whiskey, sitrep over," Jason was careful to use proper call signs even on a scrambled frequency.

"This is whiskey three niner." Jeb responded.

Colonel Fernandez and Jeb had just arrived to monitor the oil refinery, located about 3 miles north of Bennett. The defining marks of the refinery could not be missed. Three massive petroleum containers rose 40 feet into the air. The two recons had waded, climbed, and crawled almost a mile through a frozen drainage ditch to reach this observation post.

"Just made it into position. We don't see nothing yet, Jason."

Jason cringed at the use of improper procedure, and worse, his name on the radio, but he let it slide.

Both Jeb and Colonel Fernandez were using night vision scopes provided courtesy of the Stone County jail tower guards.

"The only thing we see is the night crew. Wait..."

Jeb looked again, not at the refinery itself but at the railroad tracks across the highway. Was there movement?

"Jason, I think we got something odd. Yes, I see one person, no make that two people across the highway. No, is that a vehicle?"

"Please clarify?" Jason asked.

"Hang on, Jason."

Jeb paused, then he asked the colonel, "What is that thing to the left of that reservoir by the ditch?" The two whispered, pointed, and whispered a bit more.

"Jason, somehow they are onto us. This place is an ambush waiting to happen. We count at least three armored vehicles, two behind the train tracks and one in a grove of trees north of the refinery. There are five personnel visible, and I can see the breath vapor of others in the cold. Could be several more vehicles. What do you want us to do?"

Jason thought for a moment. Somehow the mission had been compromised. Only three people knew besides him: Mosby, 1LT Ryan, and *the mayor*.

"Escape and evade. They are looking for us. Move back with no contact. Have Southwest make ready for enemy contact at home. Truck drivers in Pecan Grove are to leave their vehicles and stand down."

"Roger, wilco. Will keep it quiet, and go home. Out."

"Thanks, Jeb," Jason said, not bothering with the call sign, either.

Under a scrambled freq, Jason put out the word; "Head back to Oak Ridge and augment the sentry positions on Highway 1 and 167. Plan Delta. Relief forces maintain at the traffic light. We can expect an attack tonight, in force." DHS would want to occupy Oak Ridge and crush any remaining resistance. It would set an example, so to speak. Jason immediately got on the radio to Jacksonport and Jacksonville Air force Base. It was 3:00 a.m. He prayed there was enough time.

Breaking from the convoy, Jason quietly drove to the Wilson County Court House. The mayor had made himself a makeshift apartment on the second floor. Jason and two militia entered the courthouse and walked stiffly up the stairs.

Jason did not bother knocking. Bursting into the room, he found the mayor had been preoccupied with a blonde-haired teenage girl, no more than 14 years in age. The mayor raised up in bed like a shot, almost pulling the sheet from the naked teen. "What is the meaning of this?" the weasel of a man shouted, betraying the fear in his voice. Jason leveled his 9mm Browning at the man's midsection. His eyes were directed to the side of the bed. On a nightstand were a Singuars radio set and an encryption device that Jason had never seen before. Also on the small table was a CEOI with call signs. Flipping it over to the front page, Jason could read it even in the dim light of the room: For Official Use Only—Component Command Authority—Department of Homeland Security.

"You are under arrest, you piece of shit, for treason against the town of Oak Ridge and these United States of America." Jason paused. "And you, young lady. Get some clothes on. You should be ashamed of yourself." Jason turned and left.

As Jason was driving north to town, civilians were being mustered for

Air Plan Alpha. The civilians seemed calm enough, quite confident even, having practiced Air Plan Alpha several times. There was a good reason the plan had been practiced so frequently. There was no Air Plan Bravo.

About 4:30 a.m. a radio transmission: "Sir, they are almost in Highfield. We *can* hold Highfield Road. An entire army could not go up that hill. But I do not know how long we can hold Highway 1."

"Slow down, Soldier. Give me a SALUTE report."

The voice took a breath. "I think the first one is a Bradley, sir. The other 6 are M113s. .50 caliber machine guns mounted, it appears, sir."

Hell, another Bradley? Its computer-controlled 25mm gun alone could defeat Oak Ridge, Jason thought.

"Any visible air support?"

"No, sir."

None yet, Jason thought. If the raid at Riceland had failed to destroy a Bradley, it probably could have missed another Apache, too.

"Can you delay them? We need time."

A pause, then another voice. Australian accent. Davenport? "Sir, Highfield will give you that time."

Jason radioed Jacksonville Air Force Base again. This time it was the voice of the Air Guard commander. They were still working on a plan.

"Sir, I have an overwhelming enemy force to the north of town on Highway 1 in Oak Ridge," Jason advised. "They are hell-bent on slaughtering the entire town. Now the members of the 877th and the brave citizens of this town are calling on you to help. Sir, your only plan is to act now, or we all die. Acknowledge."

A pause. "Acknowledge."

....

The highway bypassing the small community of Highfield was wide and flat. In the daytime, there would have been no way to plan an effective ambush at close range. It was, however, night. The moon had begun to set, darkening the sky. As the armored convoy came into range, a .50 caliber machine gun, complements of Bo Hill, began chopping into the side of the M2 Bradley, yet unable to penetrate the laminate-armored vehicle. The Bradley returned fire toward the area of the nuisance with a burst of 25mm rounds, throwing up dirt and stopping the world of the militia hummer...for a moment. Somehow the Bradley had missed. Then the hummer began moving forward and down the hill, escaping a second burst from the Bradley rounds only because the hummer had stopped behind a trailer. Tracers lit up the dark, and the mobile home took the rounds full force, instantly turning it into something resembling shredded paper. Suddenly, in the dark, a person ran out in the middle of the highway, directly in front of the Bradley. He appeared to be carrying something cone-shaped, like a giant football. The Bradley continued on at 25 miles an hour, knocking the man down and running him over. But then, there was a rocking boom, and the Bradley suddenly stopped, having thrown a track. Justin Davenport, proud resident of Highfield, Arkansas, had bought Oak Ridge a little time with a shaped charge.

As if taking cue, a militia man with an AT-4 opened up at the tracked vehicle behind the Bradley. A streak of smoke pointed toward the exploding round, which hit the M113 in the tracks. Although it did not penetrate the M113's armor, the vehicle was rocked by the heavy concussion of the blast. 7.62 rounds from the Bradley secondary gunner cut the militia man down where he stood, reminding everyone that the lead vehicle was down but not out. Bo Hill's hummer-mounted .50 caliber answered in reply, peppering the Bradley yet again, instantly killing their machine gunner.

Then, the militia hummer did something unexplainable. It barreled at high-speed directly toward the disabled Bradley. When it reached the highway, it pulled a hairpin turn, and began driving directly past the convoy. It was Juan at the wheel. He was yelling something in Spanish as he sped back up. Another person, who evidently had no fear of death or dismemberment, jumped out from the hummer with a bonsai cry. It was Tim, running up on the second tracked vehicle and slamming a grenade in the open gunner's hatch. The M113 gunner was actually hit in the helmet by the grenade, only understanding what had happened the moment the grenade exploded. Not wasting time, Tim threw himself into the gunners hatch, standing on the bloody body of his predecessor. Juan piloted the hummer down the convoy line, knocking off the driver's side mirror as he drove next to the tracked vehicles. Above him, Philip was firing the .50 caliber point blank at the M113s. Metal sparked as armor-piercing rounds met heavy metal. Apparently the M113 gunners were having a hard time not targeting their own vehicles with Juan driving so close. Then, another whooshing sound of an AT4. By this time, Tim had turned the borrowed .50 caliber to the rear, and was peppering the lethal rounds down the row into the enemy convoy. The hummer had passed 4 personnel carriers, when it suddenly whipped in front of an M113, fishtailed, and just stopped. The entire driver's windshield panel had been knocked out by two .50 caliber rounds. Juan, who had been behind that windshield, was killed instantly. Philip still continued to fire away at the M113 directly facing him until he had no more ammunition. Not taken aback in the least, Philip screamed, jumped out of the hummer, and ran forward with a M4 in hand, firing it like a man insane.

It was a very desperate plan, a madman's plan, but a plan. Having lain in wait in the drainage ditch, about 20 volunteers, armed only with shotguns, rifles, pistols, and grenades, came charging from the left roadside, attacking the last two armored vehicles. The desperate aggressors pulled grenade pins as they ran, "cooking off" the grenades before throwing them. One woman was turned into a red spray as she failed to throw her grenade before it exploded.

Somewhere from behind, a red pickup drove full speed and crashed into the last armored vehicle, causing it to throw a track. A rather large, bald-headed man with a tattoo down the side of his face jumped out of pickup and climbed up the APC. He actually managed to grab the machine gun's barrel before he was shot point blank by the gunner. The dead man's torso, however, was still clinging to the machine gun. Unable to train his weapon, the gunner had no chance to survive the next assailant, a woman with bright red hair, tattoos, and a grenade. She collapsed next to her dead husband, directly on top of the gunner, screaming while pushing a grenade into the gunners hatch. A muffled pop and smoke ended both her life and every life inside the disabled vehicle.

The armored vehicles were being assaulted at point blank range by crazed attackers. Although they had swung their machine guns to fend them off, some attackers had already found cover from the APCs themselves. Two tracks tried to maneuver and turn back on the highway. Two vehicles ahead, Tim turned the machine gun upon the flanks of the fleeing vehicles. "Line those duckees up! Dammit. Line those duckees up!" Tim screamed madly. Then, as he looked north up the highway, he saw the lights. "Oh, shit." Another line of armor was coming.

"Retreat!" Tim called, blowing an air horn and running toward Juan's hummer. "Oh, God." Tim gently lifted Juan's dead body to the back seat. Then he pulled the hummer up to where Philip was lying on the pavement. It had been a costly sacrifice, Tim thought, as he picked up Philip, placing him, too, in the back. Three other defenders had miraculously survived their suicide attack. With everyone in the hummer, they moved up Highfield road, and parked in the trees, determined to defend Highfield to the last man. Tim looked at Philip, unconscious in the passenger seat. "I hope it was worth it."

Back in Oak Ridge, Jason had positioned men at 100-meter intervals along the railroad tracks. He had two surface-to-air missiles, 5 AT-4s, three claymores, and a .50 caliber machine gun to fight against the second convoy approaching: 12 M113s and probable air support. Still no answer from Jacksonport. Damn, he could have used some more Stingers. He had planned the best he could. But he felt, no, he knew it was not enough. Now he could do nothing else...except pray.

"God," Jason whispered, "I know we do not always see eye-to-eye. But if I die today, please take care of my wife and sons. Remember that I died doing what I knew to be right. Please have mercy on me...." Jason paused, wiped a tear, then clinched his fist. "But, if is Your will," Jason spoke louder. "Please lend me Your strength to defend this town. Let me kill these murdering evil bastards to the last man. So help me, God." Jason uttered the last words like an oath, a blood oath.

It was 6:20 a.m. The approaching armored column appeared about three miles distant. Jason waited. The hummer with the .50 caliber machine gun was about 100 meters to the west of the road to the front of the sentry post. Telephone poles were scattered across the road and C4 charges were ran as well. There were other surprises with explosives waiting inside the city, but if the battle got that far, it would not be a victory for Oak Ridge.

"Twelve M113s." The forward observer reported.

Then the unmistakable beat of helicopters in the distance. They were holding off for close air support.

"Wait, they are too far out. You can't hit those choppers now. 500 meters or less," Jason advised his two teams. It looked as though these were Blackhawks. Jason never thought he would be thankful for enemy Blackhawks. The choppers hovered with the moving column, offering recon and support. They had not detected the farthest rocket launcher team. On both sides of the highway, there were 2 parallel trenches chest deep and cut down the middle by another trench, forming a "double T." Fifty soldiers were on the front line. When the armor moved into a herringbone attack formation, which they should, the lines would give them hell.

With the enemy column about 500 meters distant, the attack helicopters moved forward in the light of predawn. Since the trenches had not presented themselves as a target, the Blackhawks hit targets of opportunity. The newly built sentry post was the first to dissolve in a ball of fire. Then, the fire truck parked in the Northside Grocery parking lot. After all, this was shock and awe tactics at its finest; the pilots were expecting little resistance. It was when the helicopters had passed the first street of houses, that the air horn sounded to initiate Air Plan Alpha. Three hundred civilians had been waiting behind the homes on the north side of Ellis Avenue. Simultaneously everyone fired, not at the choppers, but at the roof peak of the house in front of the choppers. One helicopter drew a tail of black smoke from its engine and erupted in a fireball somewhere on Hurd Avenue. Cheers erupted from the civilians. Although taught at almost every military institution in America, mass engagement of aircraft with small arms had almost never been practiced by American troops, perhaps because America had always had the luxury of air superiority. The second helicopter, also hit, swung out of control for a moment, and then skittered north of town. The second line of three Blackhawks, at first did not realize what had occurred, but when they had, they were set upon by the Soldiers of the 877th, firing from their trenches. Clips were emptied. Another Apache was hit, but not down. A Stinger missile fired loose, exploding it in mid-air, causing a crash of metal and fire.

The M113s were branching off in attack mode. The lead APC, however, moved ahead, attempting to cross a telephone pole obstacle set on the highway. As the telephone poles began rolling, so did the APC. Oak Ridge's sole .50 caliber Browning machine gun barked into life. On cue, the AT4s popped up, firing at tracked vehicles. The rockets were somewhat effective in, if not penetrating the side armor of the M113s, at least knocking them around. Then the C4 charges were fired on the west flank of the highway. A lead M113 had its track knocked off by the explosion. The trailing APCs had moved abreast of each other, and their infantry support was trailing behind cover of their vehicles. Small arms could do nothing to stop the APCs, so the Guard Soldiers on the west flank began retreating back out of the trench. Two Soldiers remained, with blocks of C4 in hand. One Guardsman attempted to place it on the track pads of an APC. He was riddled with bullets by supporting infantrymen. The other Guardsmen ran out of the trench, and pulled the M60 igniter as he rounded another M113. The resulting explosion killed three enemy combatants and the Guardsman, but did nothing to the APC. The choppers began strafing runs, targeting military and civilian personnel alike. Then the remaining Stinger was fired. An explosion and then only two Blackhawk helicopters remained. Two, however, were more than enough to decide the battle. The armor hit the trenches, then the explosions of C4 and shaped charges disabled two more tracked vehicles, but it was too little, too late. Oak Ridge was lost.

Jason simply refused to retreat. He had chosen to make his stand here, by the American flag. Bullets whizzed past him. It did not matter. He would die here. A bullet grazed his left cheek, burning it like fire. Another hit his rifle, shattering the stock. Jason dropped the SKS and pulled his 9mm Browning. Then a single Guard Soldier came running up toward him. Almost to Jason's side, the Soldier was cut down by enemy fire. Three more came, SSG Moses in lead, running forward, then a ragged wave. It was the Soldiers of the 877th. They would all die together, fighting to defend their families. It was altogether fitting that they do so.

Then, a sound different than the others. It sounded like a long, incredibly deafening buzz. The ground 30 yards in front of Jason erupted into an explosion of rock, pavement and dirt. Armored personnel carriers were being sawed in two, exploding. Jason was unable to move. The two remaining Blackhawk helicopters turned in midair as if to engage something yet unseen. They both exploded instantly, falling to the ground. It was as if the hand of God had reached out and crushed them. The chaos, the noise, the destruction could not have lasted any more than 10 seconds. Jason looked to the morning sky. It was an A-10 Thunderbolt, also known as the "Warthog." The aircraft flew back by, moving west, this time tipping its wings. On the aircraft's fuselage, Jason recognized to whom the aircraft belonged. Jason wept, silently thanking both God and the Arkansas Air Guard.

Oak Ridge was free, and alive that day, but the price for that freedom had been costly. Twenty-three people in Highfield had sacrificed their lives, not for some abstract sense of honor or national pride, but simply to defend their families. Another one hundred and forty-six people in Oak Ridge died for the same reason: the right to simply live their lives. The battle was over, but a war had begun.

There would be other days to follow and other battles to fight, but life would continue. Jason's son Peter would marry, and his older brother Philip would recover from his wounds. Maria would weep over the death of her husband, as Deborah would later mourn the death of Jason. But it would not be that day. That day, Jason Hamilton was going home.

ABOUT THE AUTHOR

Joe Hinds lives in Northeast Arkansas with his wife Denise.

Made in the USA
Charleston, SC
02 March 2015